Dark and Dangerous

McIntyre Search and Rescue

Book 4

by

April Wilson

Copyright © 2024 April E. Barnswell/
Wilson Publishing LLC
All rights reserved.

Proofreading by Michelle Fewer, Lori Holmes, Adelle Medhi, and Sue Vaughn Boudreaux

Cover by Steamy Designs
Photography by Wander Aguiar
Model: Soj

Published by
April E. Barnswell
Wilson Publishing LLC
P.O. Box 292913
Dayton, OH 45429
www.aprilwilsonauthor.com

ISBN: 9798328953382

No part of this publication may be reproduced, stored in a retrieval system, copied, shared, or transmitted in any form or by any means without the prior written permission of the author. The only exception is brief quotations to be used in book reviews. Please don't steal e-books.

No part of this book may be used in training any artificial intellligence tools or software.

This novel is entirely a work of fiction. All places and locations are used fictitiously. The names of characters and places are figments of the author's imagination, and any resemblance to real people or real places is purely coincidental and unintended.

Books by April Wilson

McIntyre Security Bodyguard Series:
Vulnerable
Fearless
Shane–a novella
Broken
Shattered
Imperfect
Ruined
Hostage
Redeemed
Marry Me–a novella
Snowbound–a novella
Regret
With This Ring–a novella
Collateral Damage
Special Delivery
Vanished
Baby Makes 3

McIntyre Security Bodyguard Series Box Sets:
Box Set 1
Box Set 2
Box Set 3
Box Set 4

McIntyre Security Protectors:
Finding Layla
Damaged Goods
Freeing Ruby

McIntyre Search and Rescue:
Search and Rescue
Lost and Found
Tattered and Torn
Dark and Dangerous

Tyler Jamison Novels:
Somebody to Love
Somebody to Hold
Somebody to Cherish

A British Billionaire Romance Series:
Charmed
Captivated

Miscellaneous Books:
Falling for His Bodyguard

Audiobooks by April Wilson
For links to my audiobooks, please visit my website:
www.aprilwilsonauthor.com/audiobooks

1

Jack

I killed a man today, from a mile away, lying up on a ridge shrouded by a thick forest, unseen by my target and his hypervigilant bodyguards. After calculating for wind speed and gravity, with one eye glued to the scope of my McMillan TAC-338A sniper rifle, I took my shot, ending the life of a Russian mob boss who'd attracted the attention of some very powerful people. The mob is tolerated in New York City to an extent, but Antonin Yevgeny crossed a line when he stepped on the wrong toes, and in the blink of an eye, his life was forfeited. The moment he hit the ground, his younger brother, Yuri, assumed the leadership position. We basically traded one mob boss for another. I wondered, *what's the point?*

It was a clean hit. One shot to the head, mission accomplished. Afterward, my boss congratulated me on a job well done. I went out with my buddies that night and, as I got drunk, I questioned my life choices.

And the next day, on my fortieth birthday, I resigned my position as a hatchet man—what you'd call a hitman—working for a private organization that does contract jobs for a certain US government agency that shall remain nameless. We get our hands dirty so they don't have to. It's called *plausible deniability*.

But it was time for me to go. After almost ten years in the US Navy SEALs, followed by a decade working for a shadow death squad, I was done. Ready to move on.

It had gotten too easy for me to pull the trigger—too easy for me to take a life. Yes, they were the baddest of the bad, but still, that's not who I wanted to be. Not anymore. I wanted more out of life. I wanted to settle down, establish roots, even have a family. But at the time, based on my most recent career choice, I felt like I didn't deserve more. And I wanted to become someone who did.

So I liquidated some assets and moved my money so it could be easily accessible. I paid cash for a sweet '67 black Impala—*yeah, I know, it's not the most inconspicuous of cars*—from a used car lot in Massachusetts, bought a defunct Ohio license plate from a flea market in Pennsylvania, and traded my sniper's rifle for a Glock 20 on the black market. I hit the road with little more than the clothes on my back and a bag full of burner phones.

Unfortunately, my anonymity has been blown, most likely due to a mole in my organization. Someone's been tailing me ever since the hit on Antonin. I'm guessing it's Yuri Yevgeny's men. So far I've managed to stay one step ahead of them, but eventually they'll catch up. And when they do, we'll have it out once and for all.

As long as I keep moving, I stand a chance of surviving this cat-and-mouse road trip long enough for them to lose interest in me. Theoretically, anyway. But for some reason, they never seem to be far behind.

And that makes me wonder which of my buddies is a mole.

* * *

Six months later...

It's Friday evening when I walk into *Ruth's Tavern*, a hole-in-the-wall bar located in a Podunk town in the foothills of the Rocky Mountains.

One week ago, as I was passing through Bryce, Colorado, population 829—a town so small you'd miss it if you blinked—I stopped for gas. It was after nine, and everything except the gas station and a bar was closed for the night. Gnawing hunger and the aroma of grilled meat drew me to the tavern, where I ate the best damn burger I'd had in years. That's when I first saw *her*—the most compelling woman I'd ever laid eyes on. Gorgeous, yes, but it was more than that. She radiated a power, a confidence, a no-holds barred attitude that really piqued my interest.

I figured she was about my age, early forties. She was obviously Native American, with long, silky black hair that she wore in a thick braid that hung halfway down her back. Her skin was a burnished shade of light copper-brown, her sharp eyes dark as a moonless night sky. She was dressed casually in distressed blue jeans that hugged a generous ass, a red-and-white plaid flannel shirt over a tight-fitting black tank top, and well-worn cowboy boots. This was no girl. This was a woman who'd been around the block a few times. This was a woman who knew her own mind. This was a woman I wanted to know better—much better.

That first night, I stayed until closing time—one a.m.—when she ordered us stragglers out the door. I lingered on my barstool until I was the only customer left, hoping to exchange a few words with her. The servers had left two hours prior. Besides Ruth, an older guy was still here as well as a young kid sweeping the floor.

"You too, pal," Ruth had said to me as she nodded toward the door. "It's closing time."

"Yes, ma'am," I'd said as I pulled out my wallet and laid cash on the bar. I never use credit. I never leave a paper trail.

I should have hopped in my car that night and kept driving, continued on south to Arizona on my way to Mexico, but I didn't. Instead, I backtracked a mile or so until I came to a roadside motel I'd passed on my way into town—The Lone Wolf. It was one of those old motor courts dating back to the '50s, a row of one-story white buildings with blue doors.

I walked into the office and handed the guy behind the counter forty bucks for a night. He handed me an actual key on a leather keychain. No keycards here. We're talkin' old school.

That was the first night I hadn't slept in my car in weeks.

I went back to the bar the next evening around the same time. I parked in the rear lot, in the back row away from the lights. I sat in my car for a while, just monitoring the parking lot to make sure I hadn't been followed.

After I was sure the coast was clear, I walked in through the back door, strolled down a hallway past a storage room, an office, two gender-neutral bathrooms, and lastly the kitchen, on my way to the main bar area.

The place was hopping, full of chatter, country music from an old-fashioned jukebox playing over a sound system, couples on the dance floor. While nothing fancy, the place sure had plenty of character. A hand-carved sign hanging over the bar said *HANK'S TAVERN EST. 1960*. I guess it was Ruth's place now.

The walls were wood planks, decorated with old tin signs advertising popular brands of beer and 8x10 black-and-white photographs of cowboys and horses. There were a few cowboy hats hanging on the walls, spurs, bridles, and posters featuring popular local landmarks.

The bar itself ran along the back wall, ending in a ninety-degree turn. The front and side walls were lined with booths, and there were tables positioned around a small dance floor. The floor itself was made of old wooden boards, scuffed and scarred, that had been worn smooth over the decades. A few pool tables and dart boards attracted a rambunctious crowd.

I walked the length of the bar, passing stools topped with well-worn, hand-stitched brown leather seats. Above the stools hung vintage stained-glass pendant lights. Behind the bar, a mirrored wall held shelves of liquor bottles. It was an old-timey place that probably hadn't changed much in its sixty plus years of existence.

I liked the vibe of the place, but what brought me back that second night was the woman standing behind the bar—Ruth. She was like a queen reigning over her kingdom. When I looked at her, my chest tightened and my breath caught in my lungs. I couldn't remember the last time the sight of a woman did that to me.

I've been coming back ever since, night after night, just to see her. To hear her voice. To meet her gaze and wish I were someone else—someone worthy of knowing her. Someone who had the right to walk up to her, introduce himself, and ask to buy her a drink.

But I'm not that someone. My hands are stained with blood. She deserves so much better, and no amount of wishing on my part can change that.

I've seen no sign of a husband or boyfriend. I've since learned she has a younger brother and a gang of girlfriends who stop in frequently to say hi and shoot the breeze with her. But I haven't seen any sign of a significant other. No one with an apparent claim on her personal time.

God, I want to be that man.

2

Ruth

"Guess who just walked in," Chrissy says as she walks up to the bar to pick up a tray of beer bottles. The curvy, young blonde blushes at the sight of something, or rather someone, walking into my tavern.

I hardly need to look to guess. For the past week, this guy has walked into my place every evening. He takes a seat at the far end of the bar, in the shadows, with his back to the wall. He orders the same thing every night—a double shot of whiskey, neat. The good stuff—top shelf. And then he proceeds to sit in the shadows and nurse his drink.

When my back is turned, I swear I can feel his gaze on me. It's practically palpable. After a couple of hours, he lays a twenty on the counter and walks out without a backward glance.

The man has gotten under my skin, and that's not an easy thing to do. I gave up on men years ago. Getting burned one too many times will do that to you. I've come to the conclusion I'm better off alone. Less trouble, less drama. And a hell of a lot more peace.

But this guy? He keeps coming back, and word's getting around. He's got all the single women in town in a tizzy. At least business is up. It's gotten to the point that even my girlfriends are teasing me about him, calling him my *secret admirer*. Even my brother, Micah, is razzing me about him.

When he passes by me, we make eye contact for a brief moment, but it's enough to make my pulse pick up. One look at him sends my traitorous hormones into overdrive. I may be done with men, but I'm not dead. My body still has *needs*. Just the sight of this guy stokes my fire.

He's got that *bad boy* look down pat—black leather jacket over a black T-shirt that hugs a muscular torso, black jeans, black biker boots. I can see tattoos on his neck and on the backs of his hands, and that makes me wonder where else he has some. I admit to having a weakness for ink. And he's tall, which is a big plus in my book. I'm five-ten, and he's got at least several inches on me.

My brother, Micah, is sure he's former military. I guess Micah should know. He did two tours as a helicopter pilot in the Marine Corps.

I watch out of the corner of my eye as the mystery man heads for his seat at the far end of the bar. Tonight there's someone already sitting there—a tourist from the looks of it. If he was a local, he'd know better than to sit there.

I bite back a smile, curious to see how tall, dark, and dangerous handles the situation. He walks right up to the guy, towers over him, and glares. He doesn't say a word.

He doesn't have to.

It's all I can do not to chuckle when the tourist slides off the barstool, grabs his drink, and slinks away.

This guy sure puts off powerful vibes. They're enough

to strike fear in the hearts of most men and fuel the fantasies of most women. Including mine.

"Um, Ruth? Hello!"

I snap out of it and smile at Jess, another server, who's standing across the bar from me. "Sorry, Jess. What do you need?"

"Distracted much?" She grins, knowing exactly where my attention has wandered. "I said, I need a pitcher of draft and five mugs."

Jess is a petite powerhouse of a woman, with short, dark brown hair, dark eyes, and curves that just won't quit. She's also got a mouth on her. Her low-rider jeans fit her tight as a drum, and her top is cut low, not leaving much to the imagination. I keep telling her this isn't Hooters, but she doesn't take the hint. I guess that's why she gets such good tips.

Jess nods toward the far end of the bar. "I see your hottie is here."

"He's not mine." I load a tray with mugs and then fill a pitcher with draft beer. "Here you go." Jess is no longer paying attention to me because she's too busy staring at—*oh, hell*, I don't even know the guy's name. "Jess!"

Her dark eyes snap back to me, and she smiles guiltily. "Can you blame me?" *He's fucking hot*, she mouths to me as she picks up the tray and pitcher and walks away, tossing *him* a come-hither glance over her semi-bared shoulder.

I watch for his reaction, only to find he's not even paying her any attention.

This is getting ridiculous.

It seems like every single woman in this place has the hots for this guy. Without even asking what he wants, I pour him a double, walk to the end of the bar, and set the glass down in front of him, perhaps harder than necessary.

His gaze meets mine. His irises are so dark they practically blend in with his pupils. Dark lashes. Dark hair that's a tad too long to be called short. His trim dark beard and mustache frame a pair of beautifully-shaped lips that inspire sinful thoughts. *God, I know exactly where I'd like to feel those lips.*

He reaches for the glass. "Thanks."

His voice is deliciously deep, the kind of voice a woman wants to hear whispering in her ear in the middle of the night.

For a moment, I entertain the idea of taking him home with me. No strings, just sex. I've got an itch with his name on it—the only problem is I don't even know his name.

I glance down at the hand holding that glass. His skin is tan, his fingers long and capable. There's a braided strip of leather tied around his right wrist and one of those high-tech watches on his left—the ones with all the dials and gauges. And the tattoos on the backs of his hands—*damn*.

I try not to dwell on those capable fingers and what they'd feel like on my body. Between my legs. That way lies madness.

I finally voice the question I've been dying to ask since he first showed up. "So, have you got a name?"

He looks me in the eye, but doesn't answer right away. There's a lot going on behind those eyes—it's like he's calculating the risk in answering.

"People are asking," I say with a shrug, as if I need to justify the question.

"*People?*" He raises his glass to his lips and takes a sip, still in no hurry to answer. "I don't really care what *people* think."

His voice makes me weak in the knees, and that *attitude*. "Okay, *I'm* asking."

One of his brows lifts in surprise, and he grins. "Well, in that case, it's Jack."

"Got a last name, *Jack*?"

His eyes narrow. "Is it still you who's doing the askin'?"

I nod, wondering if that makes a difference.

He says, "Jack Merchant. Pleased to meet you, Ruth."

When he holds out his hand, I hesitate a moment before taking it. All I wanted was his name, and suddenly I'm getting a lot more than I bargained for. Skin on skin contact. When my hand touches his, electricity shoots up my arm.

His palm is warm and dry, his fingertips calloused. His hand envelopes mine, but he doesn't actually shake it. He just *holds* it for a long moment, his thumb gently brushing the back of my hand. It's unsettling.

I pull my hand away. "How do you know my name?"

Never once taking his eyes off me, he nods to the front door. "It's right outside, above the door."

Of course, the sign. Ruth's Tavern.

"But how d'you know it's *my* tavern, that I'm Ruth?"

He smiles. "That's easy, darlin'. You're the one in charge here."

I see the challenge in his eyes now. *The fire.* "So, what brings you to Bryce?" It's a legitimate question. Our little town doesn't make it onto most maps. People generally pass through Bryce on their way to somewhere else, unless they're vacationing at The Lodge. With the exception of the local hiking trails, The Wilderness Lodge is the only tourist attraction for miles around.

"Just passin' through," he says, and then he takes another sip of his drink. "Do I have to have a reason?"

"Most folks do."

He grins, showing straight white teeth. "I'm on a sight-seeing trip."

I don't believe that for a second. "Fine. But keep in mind, I don't tolerate trouble in my bar. Consider yourself forewarned."

He chuckles. "Are you saying I look like trouble?" He seems amused by the thought.

I give him an arch look—the one I give my brother when he does something reckless.

He grins. "Rest assured, Ruth, I promise to be on my best behavior."

I don't know who he is, but he's got a look about him that says, *cross me and I'll gut you.* I suspect he knows how to handle himself. And because he's wearing a leather jacket inside the building, I'm pretty sure he's packing, which is against house rules. Against *my* rules. The only gun allowed in my bar is *mine*—the one I have stashed behind the counter, in a drawer beneath the cash register.

"Enjoy your evening," I say. At least now I have a name.

As I walk away, I *feel* his eyes on me, and the sensation is as palpable as a caress.

Flustered by our brief interaction, I pour a pitcher of beer and carry it across the room to the table where my friends are seated. It's Friday night, which means it's Girls' Night Out.

"I figured you could use a refill," I say as I set the pitcher on the table. Their first pitcher is nearly empty.

My five best friends are seated at this table, and they're all sneaking peeks at Jack Merchant. At least now we have a name.

"What did your secret admirer have to say?" Maggie asks when I pull up a chair and join them. Maggie Emerson owns Emerson's Grocery two doors down from my bar. "I saw you talking to him just now."

"He's not mine," I say for the umpteenth time.

"Based on the way he's watching you right now, I'm guessing he could be," she replies. "That is, if you want him. I'm pretty sure if you crook your finger at him—"

"It's hardly a *secret*," Jenny says, laughing as she refills her mug. Jenny Lopez's diner is right next door, sandwiched between my bar and Maggie's grocery store.

"He's clearly into you."

"Do you know his name yet?" asks Hannah, owner of the The Wilderness Lodge, the biggest tourist attraction around. People come from all over the world to book their outdoor excursions, everything from wilderness camping to rock climbing.

"Who cares what his name is?" Maya asks. She works for Hannah as a rock-climbing instructor. "You need his *number* so you can order room service."

"John thinks he's former military," Gabrielle Hunter says, referring to her new boyfriend. "Special ops. He said he's got that look about him. You know, hypervigilant."

Aww, my posse. God love 'em. They mean well, and I know they're just looking out for me.

"What do you really know about him?" Gabrielle asks. She's new to town, just moved here from Chicago only a month ago to take the job of restaurant manager at The Lodge.

"He looks like trouble," Maggie says as she sips from her water bottle. She's a nursing mom, so no alcohol for her.

"He's too serious," Jenny says. She sips her beer.

I lean back in my chair. "I know about as much as you guys do. He drinks whiskey and tips well." I don't mention the deep, sexy voice and the long, capable fingers."

Maya laughs. "Oh, I bet he wants to give you more than just the *tip*."

Maggie nods as the others laugh. At forty-one, she's the oldest of the group. Often, she's the voice of reason. "It's true, Ruth. We've seen the way he watches you when you're not looking."

Jenny nods. "Like he's starving, and you're a slice of cherry pie with whipped cream on top." She owns a diner, so of course she would use a food metaphor.

"Actually, I did get his name," I say, finally answering Hannah's original question. "So, you can stop calling him *hottie*."

Maya leans forward, her elbows on the table. Her dark eyes sparkle. "Tell us. It might come in handy if the sheriff starts asking questions."

"Jack Merchant. Now, how about I get you girls something to eat before all that alcohol goes to your heads?"

After making a trip to the kitchen to grab them an assortment of appetizers, I leave my friends to enjoy their food and drink, while I return to the bar.

The place is packed tonight. Not only is it a weekend night, but my bar is the only business in town that stays open after nine o'clock. Chrissy and Jess are busy nonstop, taking and filling customer orders. Tom Tanner, my assistant manager, helps me behind the bar. Casey keeps the place clean by bussing tables and sweeping the floors. The kitchen staff is hopping as well, serving up burgers, hot wings, fries, nachos, onion rings. Typical bar food.

Around ten, my friends head home.

At eleven, Jack lays a twenty on the bar and heads for the back hallway. Just before he turns the corner, we make brief eye contact, and my heart skips a beat.

He nods. *Goodnight, Ruth.*

I can almost hear the words in my head—in that voice.

At twelve-thirty, I announce the final call for drinks. There are only a few hardcore customers left in the bar at this late hour, all men, all heavy drinkers. Fortunately, they live within walking distance of the bar. I don't let customers drive if they've had too much to drink.

The kitchen has been closed since ten. Chrissy and Jess have already gone for the night. Casey's almost done sweeping the floor. Tom is mopping down the bar while I reconcile the till.

As the clock strikes one, Tom ushers the last two customers out the front door, locks up, and turns off the neon OPEN sign. I wait for him, and we walk to the rear door together. I set the alarm and lock up.

Tom is my dad's age, in his late sixties. A little shorter than me, he has a trim build, and what hair he has left is white. He's a retired ranch hand from Montana, a good guy, calm and steady, who moved down here a while back to be close to his aging mom. She passed a couple of years ago, but Tom stayed. That's lucky for me, as he's very dependable. I don't know how I'd manage without him.

"'Night, Ruth," Tom says. He waves as he walks to his rusted out navy blue Ford pick-up, keys jangling from his fingers.

"Goodnight, Tom." I unlock the driver's door of my black Jeep Wrangler, hop in, and head for home.

On my way, I pass by The Lone Wolf, a no-frills roadside motel on the edge of town. I imagine this is where Jack is staying. Besides The Lodge, it's the only accommodation around here.

It's late, and I wonder if he's asleep already. Or is he a night owl like me? I sure wouldn't mind finding out.

Ten minutes later, I pull up to my rustic, one-story log cabin that sits in a clearing in the middle of fifty acres of pristine wilderness. Hank Jackson, my paternal grandfather, built this homestead with his bare hands back in the '60s. Prior to marrying my grandmother, Hank was a recluse who lived off-grid before it was even a thing. And now it's my home.

The cabin is small and bare bones, but I wouldn't want to live anywhere else. Besides the living room and kitchen, there's a walk-in pantry that doubles as a laundry room, two bedrooms, and a full bath. Five years ago, I had solar panels installed on the roof. Before then, I had to use a noisy gas generator to make electricity. Now I have quiet power and hot running water. All the modern conveniences.

But not much else has changed since my grandfather built this place. The pine floors are the original wide planks, now well-worn after decades of use. The walls are bare logs, well insulated with chinking. The windows are double-paned to help keep the wind out. A wrought iron woodburning stove located in the living room keeps this place warm.

It suits me fine living out here where it's quiet and private. After spending my afternoons and evenings catering to the public, I like to get as far away from people as I can. The only living things out here, besides me, are birds, foxes, bobcats, mountain lions, and the occasional black bear. And, a few times a week, my brother pops in to check on me.

I let myself into the cabin and turn on a few lights to dispel the darkness. The coals in the wood stove are banked, so I open the dampers and lay in some kindling to get the fire going again. While I'm waiting for the kindling to catch, I visit the bathroom and get ready for bed. By then, it's time for me to load the stove with enough wood to last the night.

Finally, I climb into my comfy bed to read a bit. I'm in the middle of a hot romance novel. Book boyfriends are safe. They fuel my fantasies without making impossible demands on me. Without expecting me to be the kind of woman I'm not.

I don't last long. Within minutes, my eyelids are so heavy I can't keep them open.

The last coherent thought in my head before I doze off is of Jack Merchant seated at the end of my bar. I sure would like to know his story. Lately, that man is living rent free in my brain.

I can't remember the last time a man held this much interest for me. After a couple of failed relationships and one failed marriage, I've sworn off men. I'm happy being single. I've got everything I could possibly want. But for some reason I can't get this guy out of my head. A smart woman would classify him as trouble and move on.

But who says I'm smart?

3

Jack

After leaving Ruth's this evening, I drove half an hour south to Estes Park, just for something to do. While there, I stopped at a convenience store to fill my gas tank and buy some microwavable food and a few more cheap phones. Can't have too many burner phones. I went through a fast-food drive-thru to grab some late night grub and ate sitting in my car in the parking lot.

After killing time, I head to my motel, taking the long

way back to make sure no one is tailing me. So far I haven't seen any sign of Yevgeny's men here in Colorado, but I figure it's only a matter of time until they show up.

On the drive back to the motel, I pass by the tavern. It's closed, and the lights are out. I'm sure Ruth has gone home. I wonder, not for the first time, where she lives. Does she have a place here in town? Is there someone waiting for her at home? It's hard to imagine a woman like her *not* having someone.

I continue on to the motel and park in the spot farthest from my unit. Forty bucks a night for a decent mattress, a clean shower with good water pressure, a microwave, a mini fridge, an outdated TV, and Internet is a steal. It's not bad, actually, considering the price. I've had worse. And it sure as hell beats sleeping in my car in parking lots and rest areas.

Before exiting my car, I scan the parking lot, looking for suspicious vehicles. When I don't see any, I grab my purchases and head for my room. I'm glad to see the sliver of clear tape I stuck to the doorjamb is undisturbed, meaning it's likely no one broke into my room while I was out.

After letting myself in, I put the beer in the fridge and pull out one of the burner phones. It's time for my semiweekly check-in. Fortunately, Mike is a night owl, too.

Mike Roman answers my call. "This better be who I think it is."

I chuckle. "It is."

"I guess this means you're still alive."

"Last time I checked."

Mike and I served together in the Teams. He's family. A year after I left the Navy to go work for a private covert organization, he followed. The work was easy, and the pay was excellent.

"Where are you?" he asks. "Alaska? Mexico? Puerto Rico?"

I chuckle. "Try Colorado."

"Still? Are you crazy?"

"It would seem so." I hesitate, knowing he's going to rip me a new one. "I like it here."

He's quiet for a moment. "You've been there for what—a week now? Damn it, Merch! You know better. Do I have to come out there and beat some sense into you?"

"It means a lot that you care."

"Fuck you," he says without heat. "You know better than to stay in one place for too long. Move on, buddy. I mean it."

He's right, of course. "I will."

"When? Every day you delay—"

"Soon," I say, knowing I'm being an idiot.

"Look, the guys are concerned. We can—"

"No! You stay the hell away. I mean it. If I get a whiff of any of you near me, I'll shoot you myself."

Now it's Mike's turn to laugh. "Sorry, Merch, but you're no longer our team leader. You can't tell us what to do." He sighs. "Just don't get yourself killed, okay?"

"That's the plan."

The line goes quiet for a moment. And then he says, "It's not the same without you here."

My chest tightens. "Yeah, I know. Me, too." I glance at my watch. "Time's up. Later, Mike." I end the call.

With a growl, I throw the phone against my motel room wall and watch it break apart. Then I pick up the SIM card and snap it in two. Mike and I talk on a secured line, but based on how quickly Yevgeny's men catch up to me, we're starting to doubt it's all that secure. Somebody is leaking information.

After taking a piss in the bathroom, I wash my hands and brush my teeth. The last thing I do before hitting the sack is glance outside at the parking lot to check once more for any suspect vehicles. I install my improvised door jamb lock, make sure my mini surveillance camera out front is functioning, and then fall into bed.

I try watching TV for a while in an effort to decompress, to wind down. I'm having trouble getting a certain dark-haired woman out of my head.

What I wouldn't give to be a regular guy, one who could walk right up to her and ask her out.

Unfortunately, I can't be that guy. I've pissed off some real nasty assholes, and that means I can't afford a personal life. If I got involved with her, I'd be putting a target on her head.

I should have passed right on through town, but like a dimwit, I've been hunkered down in this motel room way longer than I should. At this point, I'm lucky to still be breathing. If the Russians don't manage to take me out, my buddies will come do it just on principle.

I made my bed, and now I have to lie in it. Alone.

* * *

The next morning, I head into town for some breakfast at the diner. My desire for information is superseding my common sense. I park in front of the restaurant, shut off my engine, and survey the street on the lookout for folks who look like they don't belong.

It's eight-thirty on a Saturday morning, and naturally the diner is busy. This place is probably a magnet for the locals. Next door, the bar is closed, of course, as it doesn't open until three.

As I walk into the diner, I'm immediately hit with the aroma of freshly-brewed coffee and the sweet smell of pancakes. It's a classic 1950s diner, with a black-and-white checkerboard linoleum floor, red glitter Formica tabletops, and red vinyl chairs. A hallway on the left leads to the bathrooms, and there's a jukebox on the far right wall. The walls are decorated with posters advertising combo meals and ice cream sundaes, and local flyers announce church bake sales and school fundraisers.

I quickly scan the place, making note of the points of egress as well as checking for out-of-town mobsters. The coast looks clear.

I head for the counter, where Jenny, the owner, is cutting up a pie and transferring the slices to dessert plates. She's a pretty Latina with shoulder-length dark hair, soft round cheeks, and dimples. I'd put her in her late twenties. I've seen her hanging out at the bar a few times with Ruth's other girlfriends.

When she spots me, her eyes widen in surprise. "What

can I get you, handsome?" she asks when I take a seat at the counter.

"Black coffee and the breakfast special, please."

She smiles. "Sure thing, *Jack*."

Ruth must have told her my name. So much for keeping a low profile.

"How do you want your eggs?" she asks.

"Over easy, please."

"Bacon or sausage?"

"Bacon. Crispy," I add before she can ask.

"Toast or English muffin?"

"Toast, thanks."

"Comin' right up, hun." With a wink, she walks away.

Jenny returns a moment later with a coffee pot. She turns the empty coffee cup sitting on the counter in front of me upright and fills it.

"Thanks." I reach for a discarded newspaper lying on the counter next to me. "Do you mind?"

"Help yourself," she says. "They're free to customers. Your food will be right out."

I skim the newspaper, catching an article about an upcoming fundraiser for the high school football team. Another article talks about the local search and rescue team locating a missing eight-year-old girl who'd wandered away from her family while on a hike. There's an article about a bake sale at a local church. This is small-town America. The kind of place where someone could put down roots, build a business, start a family.

"Here you go, hun," Jenny says as she sets a plate of food in front of me. "Let me know if you need anything else."

"Thanks, Jenny." She smiles in surprise when I say her name. I can't claim to be psychic, though. She's wearing a name tag.

I skim more of the paper as I eat. A hot, delicious breakfast sure beats the daylights out of eating stale pastries from a motel vending machine. Besides, it can't hurt for me to get to know Ruth's friends.

When Jenny stops by a little later to top off my coffee, I say, "You're one of Ruth's friends." I nod toward the bar next door.

"I sure am." She gazes at me expectantly, waiting for me to say more.

"She's got a nice place." *That was lame.*

"She sure does. Years ago, way before my time, mind you, it was called *Hank's Tavern*. Her granddaddy opened it in the '60s. He left it to her when he passed, and she changed the name to *Ruth's*."

Fascinating, but not exactly what I want to know. "Is she—" I'm about to ask if she's single, but right then the bell rings as the door opens, and Jenny looks past me to see who just walked in. I automatically look, too.

"Micah!" Smiling, she waves him over.

"Hey, Jenny," Ruth's brother says as he takes the stool next to me. "Coffee, please. And the special. Scrambled, bacon, and toast."

"Sure thing, sweetie." Jenny grabs the coffee pot and fills a mug for him. "Funny you should walk in now." She nods to me. "Jack and I were just talking about Ruth. You two have met, right?"

I meet a pair of obsidian eyes that are staring back hard. "Not officially, no." I hold out my hand. "Jack."

"Micah," he says as we shake hands. His gaze sharpens. "And what, exactly, do you want to know about my sister?"

"Nothing." I've never officially met the guy, but I recognize him from the bar. He's Ruth's younger brother. The resemblance is kind of hard to miss. "I just mentioned she has a nice place, that's all. The tavern, I mean."

Micah nods as he picks up his coffee and takes a sip. "I've seen you around. Are you in town for much longer?"

"No. I'll be leaving soon."

He nods. "Well, okay then. Safe travels."

"Thanks." I stand, pull out my wallet, and lay cash on the counter. "Here you go, Jenny," I call to the woman who's now standing at the kitchen window to pick up an order.

"See you, Jack!" she calls back, waving as I head for the door.

With nothing else to do, I head back to my motel room to kill some time.

Tonight, I pay my final visit to Ruth's bar. And then it's back on the road.

4

Ruth

My favorite thing to do in the morning, after eating breakfast and enjoying a cup of coffee out on my front porch, is to head across the yard to the edge of the clearing and chop firewood. Chopping and stacking wood is a constant chore. It's also my favorite form of exercise. I don't jog or do Pilates or yoga. I swing an ax.

It's only September, but the weather in this part of the Rockies is unpredictable. We can start the day off warm and sunny and end up with a foot of snow by nightfall. There's no snow in the forecast right now, but it pays to be prepared. And that means I cut, chop, and stack wood almost year around, weather permitting. I've got a lean-to beside the barn where I stack the wood so it can season.

I slip on my leather gloves and pick up the ax. Beside me is a huge pile of logs ready to be split.

I'm doing just that—the splitting part—when I hear the throaty growl of my baby brother's Harley-Davidson climbing my gravel lane.

As he rides into view, I lean the ax against the wood cart and watch him come to a rolling stop beside my Jeep, hop off, and drop the kickstand.

"Shouldn't you be at work?" I ask.

Micah owns the auto repair shop in town. He's a genius mechanic. He can fix nearly anything. He's also a part-time, on-call helicopter pilot who provides air support and evacuations for McIntyre Search and Rescue.

He removes his helmet and hangs it on a handlebar. "Just thought I'd take a break and come say hi," he says as he strolls toward me. "How's it going?"

"It's going." I grab the ax and swing hard, splitting an upright log cleanly in two. The crack reverberates through the clearing, startling a few birds.

"I can do that for you," Micah says as he leans against a tree trunk, his arms crossed over his broad chest.

I chuckle. "Thanks, but I can chop my own wood." I place another log in position and lower the ax, cleaving it in two.

Micah makes quite a picture standing there, dressed in all black—black jeans, black shitkicker boots, and black T-shirt underneath a black leather jacket. Like mine, his long black hair hangs in a single braid down his back.

Our mother was Native American, a member of the Cheyenne Tribe in Montana. She passed when Micah was just a toddler. Our father is Caucasian, born and raised here in Bryce. They met at the University of Colorado Denver, both of them studying architecture. Because we had no connection to the Cheyenne Tribe—our mother was estranged from her family—Micah and I were raised in the white world. And since our dad traveled so often for work, we ended up living here in Bryce with our white grandparents.

"So, why are you really here?" I ask. "And don't tell me it's to chop wood."

He shrugs as he pushes away from the tree. "I met your boyfriend this morning at the diner."

"I wish people would stop calling him that. I don't even know the guy."

Micah shakes his head. "That's not what I hear."

I pick up another log and set it in place. "Who have you been talking to?"

"Jenny, for one."

I laugh as I lower the ax with a loud *crack*. "Don't believe everything you hear."

"She said you chatted with him at the bar last night."

I shake my head. "I chat with a lot of people. I'm a bartender, Micah. It's in my job description."

"What do you really know about this guy?"

"Not much. Why?"

He frowns. "I don't like him. I think you should steer clear."

"Gee, thanks for the warning." I swing the ax hard. "I hope you didn't come out here just to tell me who I can and can't talk to." He sure as hell knows better than that.

"Just be careful, sis. I think he's hiding something."

"What makes you think that?"

Micah shrugs. "Just trust me on that." After giving me a guilty grin, he hops back on his bike and drives away.

I'm touched that my brother felt it necessary to come here and warn me about Jack Merchant. But I don't need to be told that Jack's trouble. He's got it written all over him. Still, there's something about the guy that intrigues me. Maybe too much.

When I've chopped a sufficient amount of wood for one morning, I stack the newly cut logs under my lean-to. Then I spend a few quiet minutes wandering through the woods and collecting kindling. It's a bit ironic that I, a total introvert, own a business that revolves around people. I need this alone time to recharge my batteries.

Once my outdoor chores are done, I head inside to take a hot shower. After getting dressed, I wash a load of clothes and hang them outside to dry. I stoke the fire in the wood stove and try reading for a while, but my mind is racing, fixating on a certain someone. Finally, desperate for a distraction, I head into town, park behind the bar, and walk down the block to Maggie's.

When I step into the grocery store, I see Maggie standing behind the check-out counter holding her one-year-old baby girl, Claire. "What's going on?" Usually, Maggie and her husband, Owen, take turns running the store while the other one stays home with the baby.

Maggie smiles as she makes goo-goo faces at her daughter. "We received a huge, end-of-season shipment of produce from Jensen Organics Farm today, so Owen came in to unload it for me."

Owen walks through the back door carrying two crates of leafy greens. He nods to me. "Hey, Ruth."

I wave to him. "Hi, Owen."

Maggie was my age when she got pregnant, quite unexpectedly, with Claire. When she and Owen met, she already had two teenage sons from a previous marriage, and she assumed her childbearing days were behind her. Surprise. After a rocky start, she and Owen are happily married now and parenting this precious baby girl together. They share everything equally—work, parenting, household chores. All of it.

Their story almost gives me hope that it's not too late for me. I'm not going to hold my breath, though. Men like Owen don't come around every day.

A man in dusty denim coveralls walks inside carrying a crate of what looks like bunches of kale. "Where do you want these, Maggie?"

"Hold on, Tom, I'll be right there," Maggie says as she hands me Claire. "Would you mind?"

"Of course not," I say as I prop the baby on my hip. I smile down at Claire, who stares up at me, eyes wide. She reaches for the turquoise pendant hanging around my neck. "You like that?"

When she tries to put it in her mouth, I pry it out of her determined little fingers and hand her a stuffed toy elephant sitting on the counter. "How about this instead?"

That seems to do the trick, because she gladly starts chewing on the elephant's trunk.

My ex-husband and I once discussed having kids. We'd actually started trying to conceive when everything unraveled right before my eyes. Chad—my ex—assumed I'd quit working at the bar when I became pregnant. In fact, as soon as we started trying to get pregnant, he suggested I sell the bar since it wasn't a "fitting business" for a wife and mother to run, and that I stay home instead and be a full-time mom.

"Does it even matter to you what I want?" I'd asked him. The tavern was a family business, inherited from my grandfather. It meant the world to me. I'd never sell it.

He'd looked at me like I was crazy. "Ruth, you can't be a bartender if you're pregnant."

"Why not?" I'd asked. "What's the big deal? I'll be serving alcohol, not drinking it."

We'd fought and fought and fought over the idea of me working in the tavern. The weird thing was, he'd never mentioned any of this to me when we were dating, or before we got married. I'd felt utterly gobsmacked.

We stopped trying to get pregnant—well, I stopped trying—because pregnancy had turned into a trap as far as I was concerned. I went back on the pill, and when he found out, he became livid.

A year later, we divorced.

I'd tried dating a few more times after Chad. But every single time, I'd ended up with a guy who resented me for having my own business, resented me for making my own money—making *more* money in fact than any of them. I don't know what they were looking for in life, but it certainly wasn't *me*.

I finally stopped trying to find Mr. Right.

"Sorry about that," Maggie says as she returns to the check-out. She holds out her hands to Claire, and Claire practically throws herself at Maggie.

"It's no problem." I smile as I watch Claire pop her thumb in her mouth and lay her head on Maggie's shoulder.

"It's naptime," Maggie says. "Owen will be done helping Tom unload the truck soon, and then he'll take her home and put her to bed."

I reach out to stroke the back of Claire's tiny hand,

which is grasping Maggie's shirt. "I should go now," I say past a painful knot in my throat. "I need to restock the bar before we open."

Maggie walks me to the door. "Thanks for stopping by. I'll see you Friday for girls' night out, if not before."

I take my leave and pass by the diner on my way back to the tavern. I catch Jenny's gaze through the windows and wave to her. She waves back as she tries to do three things at once. It's the lunch rush hour, so I won't bother going in. She's got her hands full at the moment.

I walk into the tavern around two—an hour before we open. I like this quiet time in the bar, when it's just me here, at least for a little while. The kitchen staff will arrive soon to do their prep work.

A scheduled weekly delivery truck pulls up to the back door, and I meet the driver outside. While I'm lugging in a couple dozen boxes and cases of everything from beer to paper towels to food ingredients for the kitchen, Tom arrives.

"You want me to do that, Ruth?" he asks, always the gentleman.

"Thanks, but I've got this. Why don't you restock the bar and get the cash register ready?"

By three, I've got everything carried in and distributed

properly. Tom turns on the neon OPEN sign in the front window and unlocks the doors.

5

Jack

I'm about out of clean clothes, so mid-morning I shove what little clothes I have into my rucksack in preparation for making a run to the nearest laundromat, which is in Estes Park.

Just as I'm about ready to leave, there's a knock on my door.

I tuck my Glock into the back waistband of my jeans and glance out the peephole at Ruth's brother.

He knocks again.

I should ignore him, but curiosity gets the best of me. Why's he here? To warn me away from his sister? I'd like to see him try.

I open the door and meet his gaze head on.

Unflinching, he stares right back. The guy's got balls, I'll give him that.

"What branch did you serve in?" I ask, recognizing a fellow soldier when I see one.

"Marines."

"Combat experience?"

He nods. "Two tours in Afghanistan as a chopper pilot. You?"

"Navy." He doesn't need to know the details. "What do you want?"

Micah's jaw clenches. I've pissed him off. Good.

"I'm here to give you a friendly warning," he says.

I almost laugh. "I'm listening."

"Stay the hell away from my sister. I don't know what your game is—"

"I'm not playing any games."

"Just stay away from her."

I can't fault the guy for looking out for his sister. "Don't worry. I'm leaving soon. I'll be gone before you know it."

"Make sure you are."

I watch him climb on his bike and ride away. I could be pissed that Micah thinks he has the right to warn me off his sister, but I'm not. I'm actually glad Ruth has someone watching over her.

* * *

I load my car and head to Estes Park to do laundry, taking my time, going out of my way to change up my route and make sure no one's following me.

After I toss all my clothes in a washer, I sit out of the line of sight from the street and kill time reading the latest Jack Reacher book on my phone. I drop some money into a couple of ancient vending machines and indulge my weakness for salty junk food and ice-cold Coke.

While my clothes are drying, I use my phone to log into a secure site where I can leave a message for Mike and the guys. My old team—four of them. I sure miss those guys.

Jack – I'm leaving Bryce tonight, heading to New Mexico.

After logging out of the message board, I sit and stare at a bulletin board on the laundromat wall, at the myriad of notices pinned to it. My mind wanders back to Bryce. It's noon now, and the bar opens in three hours. Maybe

I'll stop in one last time this afternoon, just to see Ruth once more and say goodbye. I hate the idea of leaving town and never seeing her again, never having a chance with her. But it's just too risky for me to stay. As long as there's a contract out on me, everyone I'm around is in danger.

Once my clothes are dry, I fold everything and shove it all into my rucksack. Then I hop in my car and head back to town. I return to my motel room and kill time lifting barbells and later going for a hike along a trail not far from the motel. I'm still trying to get acclimated to this altitude.

After showering, I drive over to the tavern just as it's opening. The parking lot in the back is starting to fill up, and customers begin filing inside for a late lunch or an early dinner.

I follow them inside, stopping short when I spot Ruth walking out of the storage room carrying three cartons of beer bottles.

She practically runs into me, her eyes widening when she spots me. "Sorry." She takes a step back. "I didn't see you."

"Let me help you." I take two of the cartons from her before she has time to protest. I realize she doesn't actually need my help, but I want to do something for her. Even something this small.

"If you insist." She starts off down the hallway, toward the bar, her eyes narrowing as she glances back at me.

"What are you doing here so early?"

"I thought I'd grab some lunch."

She nods. "Have a seat at the bar."

After setting the two cartons of beer on the counter, I continue along to my usual seat at the far end. A moment later, she's standing across the bar from me, holding out a laminated sheet of paper. "The lunch menu."

"Thanks." I give it a cursory glance even though I already know what I want. "I'll take a burger and onion rings."

She nods. "Coming right up. Anything to drink?"

"Beer. Something local. Whatever you recommend."

"Got it."

I watch as she puts my order in at the kitchen window. She proceeds to wait on a few more customers, giving me a chance to observe her.

It's not long before she brings me my food and an icy cold bottle of Fat Tire Amber Ale. She pulls an opener from her apron pocket, pops the cap, and hands it to me.

"Thanks." I take a sip. "Nice. So, Ruth." I realize I

just like saying her name. "Mind if I ask you a personal question?"

She looks surprised. "Okay. Shoot."

"Are you single?" I have no business asking, but it's eating at me.

There's a hint of a smile playing on her lips. "To answer your question, yes. I'm single." And just as I'm about to reply, she cuts me off. "And before you say another word, the answer is no. I'm not interested." And then she turns and walks away.

Ouch. That was fast. I didn't even get a chance to ask her.

After finishing my lunch, I don't bother waiting for a check. I leave plenty of cash on the counter and head out the way I came. Ruth's nowhere in sight, and I'm disappointed I won't have a chance to say goodbye. I guess it doesn't matter since it appears I never had a chance with her anyway.

The door to the storage room is open, and as I pass by, I glance inside just as Ruth attempts to pull a large cardboard box off a high shelf. The box must be heavy, because she's clearly struggling.

I walk up behind her, reach up, and grasp the box. "Allow me."

Startled, she looks back at me, and for the briefest moment, I see a myriad of emotions flit across her face—a mixture of annoyance, surprise, and anticipation—which makes me think maybe she's not as disinterested as she claims.

We're standing just inches apart, and she looks me directly in the eye. I can feel her body heat. When I catch her scent—something hot and spicy—my gut tightens. I set the box on the floor.

"Thanks," she says, her voice little more than air.

Her cheeks are flushed, her dark eyes bright. I glance down to see her chest rising as she catches her breath.

"I'm leaving town tonight," I tell her. "So, I guess this is goodbye."

"Oh." She actually looks disappointed. "I guess it is." She looks like she wants to say more, but she doesn't.

I hate the idea that this is it, that I won't ever see her again, so I decide to go out on a limb. "I'd really like to come by the bar one last time this evening to buy you a drink."

She swallows hard, but doesn't look away. If anything, her gaze is even more direct. "Since this is my bar, it's my booze. I don't need anyone to buy me a drink."

Grinning, I reach out and tug on her braid, feeling vindicated when the flush on her cheeks deepens. "Okay, fine. How about *you* buy *me* a drink?" Throwing caution to the wind, I lean in and kiss her. Just a light peck on her lips.

Her eyes widen, but she doesn't pull away. Or slap me. I see that as a good sign.

"I'll take that as a yes," I say, not giving her a chance to shoot me down. "I'll see you tonight." Before she can even form a reply, I turn and walk out.

When she doesn't holler at me, or cuss me out, I smile. Looks like I have a date tonight.

* * *

"What in the hell are you still doing there?" Mike asks when I call him that afternoon. "What's so special about this place that you'd risk your safety by hanging around?"

I chuckle. "The scenery."

"Really? And does this scenery have a name?"

"Ruth. She owns the local tavern."

"You have no time for women, my friend. You need to hit the road. You can get laid later."

"Relax. I'm leaving tonight, after she buys me a drink."

The timer on my watch goes off. We keep our calls to a

minimum. "Bye, Mike."

"Let me know when you've left."

"Yes, dad," I say.

After ending the call, I change into sweats and sneakers and go for another run. I'm not used to working out at this elevation, and it's harder than I expected. Two miles later, I'm gasping like an old man who just walked up five flights of stairs.

After my run, I grab a shower, then I crash for a while and read. Anything to occupy my mind so I stop checking the time. I think I'll show up at the bar just before closing. There won't be a lot of people there that late, which means I can have Ruth to myself for a few minutes.

When I kissed her earlier this afternoon, she didn't slap me or tell me off. No, she actually smiled. Maybe she's more into me than I thought.

6

Ruth

When Jack doesn't show up this evening at his usual time, I find myself sorely disappointed. I guess he changed his mind about having a drink with me. Honestly, that's fine. The last thing I need is the complication of a man hanging around, getting ideas, or developing expectations. The evening progresses as normal. I only have to kick out two guys for disorderly conduct.

"Where's Jack?" Chrissy asks me around ten, when he

still hasn't shown up.

Apparently, everyone knows his name now.

I shrug. "No idea. Keeping track of him is not my job." I meant it when I told him I don't need a man to buy me a drink. I don't need a man for anything. But when I think back to earlier today, when he practically pressed himself against me in the storage room and kissed me, I realize even though I don't *need* a man, it might be nice to *have* one for a change.

I certainly wouldn't kick that man out of my bed.

Still, disappointment gnaws at me all evening, to the point that both Tom and Jess keep asking me if I'm okay.

"I'm fine!" I snap at both of them.

At half past twelve, I announce the last call for drinks. There are only three guys in the place, all heavy drinkers who will stay until one of us kicks them out. Chrissy and Jess have already gone home for the night. Casey finishes sweeping the floors and clocks out. Tom wipes down the bar while I cash out the till.

Just a few minutes before closing time, Tom nudges me with his elbow. "Look who's here."

I watch Jack enter the bar from the rear hallway. He's wearing blue jeans for a change and a white button-down shirt, open at the neck. His sleeves are rolled up, revealing muscular forearms, tanned skin, and partial glimpses of his tattoos. *Hello, bad boy.*

He looks different. Almost dressed up.

"You came," I say, feeling caught off guard. His smile takes me by surprise.

"I told you I would. We have a date."

"I wouldn't exactly call it a date. It's just one drink."

"Po-tay-to, po-tah-to." He takes a seat at the center of the bar, not content to hide in the shadows tonight, and nods to Tom. "Evenin', Tom."

Tom returns the nod. "Evenin', Jack." And then Tom turns to me. "You want me to stay, Ruth?"

Of all people, Tom should know I don't need protection. He's seen me throw guys bigger than me out of my bar countless times. "No, Tom. You can go. I'm fine." Actually, I'm better than fine now.

Before I can ask Jack if he wants his usual, a local guy by the name of Lloyd walks up to the bar. Or, more accurately, I should say he staggers up to the bar. "One more for the road, Ruth," he says, slurring his words.

Lloyd lives just two blocks away, but he's so wasted one of us will have to give him a ride home. He's in no shape to walk alone.

"Sorry, pal. The bar's closed. I already announced last

call."

"But I didn't hear ya say it," he says with a pout. "Just one more, Ruth, please."

"No, Lloyd. I'm sorry. You've had—"

Lloyd's an aggressive drunk. He lunges across the bar and grabs hold of my shirt. "I said—"

Jack shoots to his feet, but before he jumps in, I grab Lloyd's hand and twist his wrist. With a sharp cry, he lets go of my shirt.

"What the hell, Lloyd!" Tom says, glaring at the drunk man.

"Lloyd, you need to go home and sleep it off," I say as I release his hand.

"I'll take him," Tom offers, scowling as he removes his apron.

One of our regulars, Eugene, raises his hand. "I'll take him," he says. "I pass right by his house on my way home. It's no trouble."

"Thanks, Eugene," I say.

Tom walks Eugene, Lloyd, and everyone else who's still here out the back door. Then he returns to the bar. "You, too," he says to Jack. "We're closing up now. You'll have to come back tomorrow."

"It's okay," I say, patting Tom on the shoulder. "I invited Jack to come by for a drink."

My assistant manager frowns. "Are you sure about this, Ruth?" he asks as he stands in the open doorway. He lowers his voice. "I don't like leavin' you here alone with this guy. We know nothing about him."

"If he causes any trouble, I'll shoot him, I promise."

Tom frowns, not appreciating my joke. "Call me if there's any trouble. Or better yet, call the sheriff."

I nudge him toward the back door. "I will. Now stop worrying and go home."

After locking up, I return to the bar, where Jack is seated once more. "Sorry about all that," I say. "Now, where were we? What can I get you?"

He gets off his barstool and walks around to the back side of the bar and shoos me to the other side. "I'm the one buying you a drink, remember? What can I get you?"

When the corner of his lip quirks up in a grin, I decide to let him play bartender. "Okay." I walk around to the other side of the counter and take a seat. "I'll have a Jack and Coke."

"Cute." He grins as he grabs a tall glass from the rack overhead, flips it in the air, and catches it effortlessly. He fills it with ice, grabs the bottle of Jack Daniels off the shelf behind him, and pours a generous splash. Finally, he fills the glass with Coke and slides it across the counter to me.

I take a sip and nod in approval. "Not bad."

He chuckles. "How hard can it be?" He makes one for himself. "A little whiskey, ice, and Coke. It's not rocket science."

"Yeah, but you got the ratio right. Are you looking for a job? I could use another bartender." That's not entirely true, but suddenly I like the thought of keeping him around a little longer.

I must have caught him off guard.

He smiles. "Seriously? You'd offer me a job?"

"Sure. Why not? You seem like a capable guy."

He smiles, but it quickly fades. "I appreciate the offer, Ruth. I really do. But I'm leaving town in the morning."

"I see." I shrug, determined not to let him see my disappointment. He's the first one to pique my interest in a long time. "Suit yourself."

He holds his glass out to me. "A toast to what might have been." There's a flash of heat in his dark eyes.

I tap my glass against his. "I'll drink to that." I take a good long sip of my cold drink, hoping it will cool me off in the process.

We end up staring at each other, and the undercurrent running between us is palpable. I realize I don't want him to go. And the intensity in his expression leads me to think he doesn't want to go either.

Jack sets his glass down and walks around the bar. He swivels my seat so I'm facing him, and then he nudges my knees apart and steps between them. Immediately, my body tightens. Heat rushes through me, and my pussy clenches hard. Why in the world do things start to get good just as he's *leaving*?

I meet his gaze, which is dark and heated and hungry.

He cups the back of my head. "God, I wish I didn't have to go."

I step out on a ledge. "Then don't."

"I have to." He swallows hard, his Adam's apple bobbing. "There's so much—" He stops mid-sentence and changes gears. "I'd really like to kiss you, Ruth."

His question hangs in the air between us.

Figuring I have nothing to lose, I lay my palms on his chest. "Who's stopping you?"

He winces. "The problem is, if I start kissing you, then I won't want to stop."

My breath catches in my chest, and heat pools between my legs. My breasts are aching, and he hasn't even touched me, not really. My body is hungry for something

DARK AND DANGEROUS 61

it hasn't had in a very long time. "Again, who's stopping you?"

"I'm leaving," he reminds me. "I don't want you to get the wrong idea."

"I know. I heard you." I slide my hands down his torso and around to grasp his ass and pull him closer, flush against my body. His hips are cradled between my open legs, his erection pressing against my heated core.

"You can stay a few more hours, right?" I'm not against a one-night stand. In fact, it's probably better this way. I don't need the complication of a man in my life. I've got everything I need, everything I want. Except for *this*. I want *him*. Right now.

"Where?" he asks.

"I have an apartment upstairs."

His eyes widen. "You're serious."

"I am."

He reaches for his drink and takes a big swig. "Lead the way."

7

Ruth

Jack follows me down the hallway toward the rear entrance. Between my office and the rear entrance is a door marked PRIVATE. I open it, revealing a dark, narrow staircase. I flip on the light.

"After you," he says, motioning for me to proceed.

Jack follows me up the narrow wooden steps to a dimly-lit landing that leads to a single door. There's a welcome mat in front of the door, and beside it sits a small metal table holding a vase of plastic daisies.

"Cute," Jack says as he fingers one of the fake flowers. "That's my attempt at trying to make it look more homey." I frown. "Interior design is not my strong suit."

Jack chuckles as I open the door. We step inside, and I turn on the lights. At least the inside of the apartment is half decent. Two large windows along the exterior wall let in moonlight. During the day, it's actually quite sunny in here.

"This is my home away from home," I say. "I use it on nights when the weather's too bad to drive home."

It's a small, one-bedroom apartment, with just a kitchenette, a sitting area, a bedroom, and a bathroom. It's barebones, but it's comfortable.

After closing the door behind us, I head for the bedroom. Jack follows.

Like the rest of the apartment, the bedroom has just the essentials—a double bed and a nightstand. There's a small closet with a few garments hanging inside. There are extra pillows and bedding on a shelf above the clothes rod.

"Shit," he says suddenly. "My condoms are in my car. I'll run out—"

"Don't bother. I've got some." I open the bedside drawer, pull out a packet, and toss it on the nightstand.

He grins, shaking his head. "Just one?"

I give him an arch look. "You're that confident?"

"I hope once won't be enough for you. I know it won't be enough for me." He stalks toward me and pulls me flush against him. One of his arms snakes around me, and with his free hand, he cups my face and gazes into my eyes. "Have I mentioned how incredibly beautiful you are?"

"No." In my experience, men compliment women when they want something from them, and they rarely say what they mean. I've been burned too many times. "I already said *yes*, Jack. You don't need to butter me up."

He laughs. "I'm not. I mean it."

I slip my arms around his waist. "How about less talking and more kissing, before I change my mind?"

His smile widens. "Yes, ma'am."

Cupping my face in his hands, he gazes into my eyes, as if searching for something. "You are beautiful," he says, "but when I first saw you, it wasn't your looks that held me captive. It was your strength. The way you carry yourself. Your confidence. That's what attracts me to you."

My heart skips a beat, and I wonder if he's a mind reader. He hardly knows me, so how in the world can he know the words I long to hear? That he's not intimidated by me.

When his mouth settles over mine, his lips caressing and molding to mine, I imagine a tug between us, connecting me to him. I brush aside the fanciful notion and focus on the feel of his mouth, his lips, his wicked tongue.

I grasp his arms and marvel at the firmness of his biceps—hard as steel beneath my fingers. His body is temptation itself—every muscle, carved and hewn. His fingers, so long and strong, so capable. I imagine how those calloused fingertips would feel on my breasts, between my legs.

As he deepens our kiss, stealing my breath and making me dizzy in the process, I take matters into my own hands and start unbuttoning my shirt. His breath hitches in his throat, followed by what I can only describe as a growl.

He stares as I shrug off my shirt and then reach behind me to unsnap my bra. That, too, falls to the floor. His heated gaze lands on my breasts.

"Are we doing this, or what?" I ask when he just stares at me.

"Hell, yes, we are," he says as he starts unbuttoning his

own shirt. "By the way, it's been a while for me, so please don't judge me on technique." He winks at me. "At least not the first time."

It's a race then, to see how fast we can both get undressed.

The bedroom is shrouded in darkness, but the door's open, and the light in the living room is on. It's enough light to see by. It's my turn to stare now as Jack's shirt falls to the floor, revealing broad shoulders and well-defined arm muscles.

His chest is a work of art, all sinewy muscles and tanned skin. It's a man's body, rough and sexy as fuck. I lay my hands against his chest, feeling his warmth. I give in to the temptation to slide my palms up to his shoulders, and then around his neck.

He's watching me ogle him, but I don't care. I greedily look my fill. If I'm going to have only this one night with him, I want to remember every moment. Stepping closer, I cup his face, then slide my fingers into his hair. When I dig my nails lightly into his scalp, gripping his hair, he closes his eyes and groans.

When I press my mouth to his, he sucks in a breath and opens his mouth, nudging my lips open as well. As he deepens the kiss, he palms my breasts, cupping them in his warm hands. He brushes my nipples with his thumbs, making them tighten swiftly into hard peaks. A jolt of electricity streaks from my breasts down to the throbbing spot between my legs. Already I'm aching and wet, and we've hardly started.

He draws me closer, my bare breasts pressing against his firm chest. One arm snakes around me, and with his free hand, he grasps the nape of my neck, cupping it firmly and sending shivers down my spine.

His mouth covers mine once more, and a deep groan rumbles in his chest as his tongue swipes against mine.

He tastes like whiskey and Coke, and he smells divine—like heat and fire and man. His hands are strong and sure, and he clearly knows what he's doing. I think that talk earlier about technique was just for show.

I gasp in surprise when he scoops me up and carries me to the foot of the bed, sitting me down. He crouches on the rug in front of me and removes my boots and socks, his fingers working quickly and sure. Then he rises and gently pushes me onto my back. His fingers make quick work unfastening my jeans and lowering the zipper before he tugs them and my underwear down my legs.

Suddenly, I'm naked and shivering in the cool, night air.

"Don't worry, I'll warm you up," he says as he kicks off his shoes and peels off his socks. He unfastens his own jeans and lowers the zipper. To my surprise, he leaves them on. Then he kneels at the foot of the bed and slips between my legs, throwing them over his shoulders.

Well, he's not wasting any time.

He moves in, holding my gaze with his the entire time, as if he's gauging my reaction. When his tongue touches me, my hips rocket off the mattress. With a chuckle, his hands bring me back down.

It's been a long time since I let a man get this close to me. He's definitely encroaching on my personal space, but surprisingly, I'm okay with it. I want his mouth on me. I want it all.

He takes my silence as acquiescence and resumes what he started. His mouth is hot and hungry, bold and demanding. My body writhes beneath his assault, my lungs billowing. I fist the comforter beneath me, tugging on the material as I squirm like a fish on a hook. *Holy fuck!*

His wicked tongue knows exactly how to drive me wild, and by the time his finger joins in the action, rimming my aching wet opening, I'm whimpering like a virgin on her wedding night. "*Jack!*"

He's relentless, driving my arousal higher and higher until my thighs are trembling, my belly quivering. My chest heaves as I try to catch my breath. My pleasure climbs until a climax slams through me. It's intense and wild and devastating. I swear I see stars. As I cry out shamelessly, I reach for him.

He shoots to his feet and shoves his jeans and underwear down his legs. Then he kneels on the bed and draws me higher up the mattress so my head falls onto a pillow.

He grabs the condom packet, rips it open, and sheaths himself with quick, practiced expertise. Then he's looming over me, using his knee to nudge my legs open wide enough for him to slip between them.

As he lifts one of my legs, opening me wider, he leans down and kisses me, his mouth stealing my breath and sealing our lips together.

Kneeling, he uses his free hand to position himself at my drenched opening. He presses in, burying the head of his erection, and then he props a hand on the mattress to keep his weight off me. Slowly, he thrusts, sliding deeper, an inch at a time, pulling out, then sliding back in, letting my arousal ease the way as he slowly stretches me.

"Okay?" he gasps, nailing me with his gaze.

All I can do is nod. It's been a while for me, and Jack's a big guy. But I love how he fills me so perfectly.

Once he's all in, he starts to move, slowly at first, but then picking up speed. His thrusts grow stronger, and now he's powering into me, swift and deep. His chest is heaving, as is mine. With a grunt, he sinks deep inside me, and then, grasping my hips, he turns us so I'm sitting astride him. Still, he does the work, raising and lowering me with his powerful hands. I press my hands to his chest to balance myself. In this position, it's easy for me to find the right angle so the head of his cock strokes my sweet spot.

I come a second time, which shocks the hell out of me. He follows right behind me, arching his back as he drives himself deep inside me. He thrusts violently, the sounds coming from him guttural and deep. Gradually, his thrusts slow, and I collapse forward onto his chest, sucking in a lungful of air.

His arms come around me, and he holds me close. We're still joined, and I can feel the lingering pulses as he continues ejaculating.

Finally, he slides out of me, lowers me to his side, and slips out of the bed to disappear into the bathroom to dispose of the condom. A moment later, I hear the water running.

Just as he comes out of the bathroom, I slip in there to take care of business. When I return to bed, he lifts the covers in an invitation for me to slip in beside him.

Jack rolls to face me and hikes one of my legs up over his hip, pulling me close. He leans in for a kiss. "I am officially wiped out."

Grinning, I say, "I guess, at your age, it's not surprising."

He returns my smile, then brushes his nose against mine. "Funny. Please tell me there are more condoms."

My heart skips a beat. "Yes."

"Good. Let me sleep a few hours first."

"It's pretty presumptuous of you to assume I want more." But who am I kidding? Of course I want more.

He cocks an eyebrow at me. "Are you saying you don't?"

A soft laugh slips out. "No."

He nods. "Didn't think so. You came twice. I counted." Then he realizes the living room light is still on, bleeding into the bedroom. "Damn it." He gets up and walks out of the bedroom, giving me an unobstructed view of his taut backside. After turning off the light, he returns to bed.

This time he rolls me over and spoons me from behind, sliding one leg between mine and curling his arm over my waist. He tucks me in close, his softened penis nestled against my ass.

He's being presumptuous again, but I don't point that out. I kind of like it.

Jack meant it when he said he was wiped out. His breathing changes quickly as he falls asleep, leaving me wide awake.

I can't believe I let him—a virtual stranger—fuck me. All I know is his name. I know nothing else about him, not where he's from, where he's going. Nothing. He could be a criminal for all I know, an ex-con even. And I just rode him like a cowgirl. *What the hell is wrong with me?*

8

Jack

I wake up around seven, alert as I take in my surroundings. Memories of last night come flooding back. The feel of Ruth in my arms, her mouth, her taste, her sweet arousal. She shifts in my arms, making a soft sound that goes straight to my dick. I'm already hard.

When I press my lips against the back of her head, she stirs.

"Good morning," I say.

Groaning, she stretches. "It is," she says as she pushes her ass into my crotch, pressing those soft round globes against my morning erection.

Okaaay. That's an invitation I wasn't sure I'd get this morning. Passion and desire in the heat of the night is one thing, but sometimes people come to their senses in the morning. And in case I wasn't getting the message, she reaches back, wraps her fingers around me, and squeezes.

That's all the green light I need. I roll over to grab another condom packet from the nightstand drawer. Quickly, I roll it on.

I toss the covers aside, uncovering both of our naked bodies. Early dawn light filters through the sheer curtains of an east-facing window, giving me enough light to see what I'm doing. Not that I need to. It's just a bonus.

I roll Ruth onto her side again, so that she's facing away from me. Then I tuck my arm around her waist and slide my fingers between her legs. Damn, she's still wet from last night. Another bonus.

I slip a finger between the lush lips of her pussy and start teasing her clit. The moment I touch that little piece of flesh, she cries out softly, arching her back and pressing her head back against my shoulder. I lean over and kiss her throat, placing an open-mouthed kiss right over her pulse point, and apply gentle suction. Yeah, I'm going to leave a mark. After I'm gone, I want her to look in the mirror and think of me. Remember this night. Remember *us*.

I shove away any thoughts of what might have been and focus on the here and now. We're here, the two of us, in this bed, and I plan to make the most of it. I sure as hell want to give her something to remember me by.

With my thumb, I draw lazy circles around her clit, teasing her, ratcheting up her desire. She gasps, arching her neck as she grabs my hand, not in an effort to stop me, but to urge me on.

Damn!

A woman who knows what she wants and isn't afraid to ask for it is a helluva turn on.

I stroke her to climax, growling in her ear when she cries out as her long legs stiffen. That's three times now, not that I'm counting.

I lift her leg and drape it over my hip, opening her up so I can enter from behind. She moans when I press into her, pushing slowly until I'm balls deep inside her. She lets out a heavy sigh as she presses her head against my shoulder. She turns her face to me, and I angle my mouth over hers, stealing the sexy sounds she makes as I withdraw and shove myself back in to the hilt.

She reaches back to grasp my ass, her nails digging deep.

I still my movements. "Did I hurt you?"

"Good God, no," she says, laughing softly. "Don't you dare stop."

I power into her, thrusting hard and deep. She's with me every second, pushing back into me, deepening our connection.

I hold out as long as I can, reveling in the feel of being buried inside her scorching wet heat. Fire screams down my spine to my balls, which tighten almost painfully. I come hard, seeing stars again.

Still nestled deep inside her, I nuzzle her neck and revel in the pleasure of being buried in her tight channel. We're both sleepy and sated, and I smile when she dozes off once more in my arms.

I need to get up and dispose of the condom. Hell, I need to *leave*. I've already stayed too long.

When I tighten my hold on her, she makes a soft, sleepy sound, which makes it even harder for me to pull away. I close my eyes and bury my lips in her hair, allowing myself just a few more minutes with her.

The fact that I don't want to leave is all the more reason why I should. I can't risk staying.

Reluctantly, I slip out of her body and head to the bathroom to clean up and dispose of the condom. After I dress quietly in the early morning light, I sit on the side of the bed and watch her sleep for a while longer.

I don't want to go. I want to crawl back in that bed with her. I want to be there when she wakes up, have breakfast with her, spend the day with her.

God, how I wish things could be different.

"Goodbye, Ruth," I whisper.

Silently, I let myself out of the apartment and out of the building, locking the doorknob behind me on my way out.

* * *

Only an hour later, as I'm packing up my meager belongings in preparation to check out of my motel room, there's a knock at the door. I check the peephole and find Micah standing outside looking pissed. Surely he can't know I spent last night with his sister. Not this soon.

I unlock the deadbolt and the chain and open the

door.

Before I can get a word out, he says, "There was a guy at my shop this morning asking questions about you."

My heart skips a beat. "I see."

"He's not from around here. I just thought you should know."

I imagine not. "Where's he from?"

"Originally? By the accent, I'm going with Russia."

Well, fuck. My window to leave Bryce, Colorado just closed. "Thanks for the intel. What did you tell him?"

"I told him nothing. Look, man, I don't know what you're mixed up with, but you need to go before you bring trouble down on my sister's head."

"I'm not mixed up—" *Oh, hell. It's too complicated to explain.* "I'm going." I nod toward the Harley parked in front of my motel room. "You should go." Realizing he might have been followed here, I scan the parking lot.

He looks me in the eye for a long moment, then turns on his heel and starts for the bike. I watch as he straddles the seat and reaches for his helmet. "One more thing," he adds with a look back at me.

I wait for the other shoe to drop. "What's that?"

"Stay the hell away from my sister."

"Yeah, I hear you."

Micah starts the engine and backs out of the parking spot. I watch him ride away.

Back in my motel room, I dig out a burner phone and call Mike.

"Tell me you left town," he says.

"Hello to you, too."

"I'm serious, Jack."

"Honest, I was just about to leave. In fact, I'm packed and ready to go. But it's too late now."

"What are you talking about?"

"Let's just say a concerned citizen stopped by to inform me there's someone with a Russian accent in town asking questions about me."

"Fuck." Mike makes a frustrated groan. "I'm still trying to figure out who's leaking info to Yevgeny."

"I hate to state the obvious."

"I can't believe one of our guys would turn on you, not after everything we've been through together."

"They're the only ones who know my whereabouts."

"Well, it's not me, damn it," Mike says.

"I never thought it was." I trust Mike Roman with my life. "So it has to be one of the others—Aleksa, Diego, Lenny."

"It's not Aleksa," Mike says. "I'd stake my life on it. He

wouldn't betray you."

"That leaves Diego and Lenny."

Mike blows out a frustrated breath. "Now what?"

"I can't leave town, not with one of Yevgeny's men here. I can't put Ruth in danger. It needs to end, here."

"Then I'm coming out there. You're going to need backup."

"No—"

"Don't waste your breath arguing with me, Jack. I'll be there as soon as I can. Since I'll need to bring a lot of firepower with me, ammo and gear, I'll have to drive. I'm in Kansas City, so it's about a ten-hour drive. I'll leave within the hour."

"I'm done running, Mike. I'm taking a stand here. We're going to have it out with these guys once and for all. I can't leave this town vulnerable. I can't leave Ruth in danger. I *won't*."

"So, you kill Yuri—assuming he comes out there himself—and then what? The next to take over the organization puts out a hit on you too? When's it going to end?"

"I don't know. I'll deal with that when the time comes. Right now, I have to make sure Ruth is safe."

Mike chuckles. "I was hoping you'd settle down one day, but this isn't what I had in mind."

After I get off the phone, I check out of my motel room in an effort to remove any traces of myself from town. I head straight for the tavern, thinking Ruth might still be there, but when I pull into the rear parking lot, it's empty. She must have gone home. The only problem is, I don't know where she lives.

So I drive over to Micah's auto repair shop, park in front of the office, and walk inside to find an elderly white-haired lady sitting behind a desk.

"Can I help you?" she asks me, staring openly.

"Is Micah around?"

She nods to an open doorway. "He's in the shop."

I walk into the auto shop, which smells like automotive oil. I spot Micah standing beneath a minivan that's up on a lift, staring up into the engine compartment.

"Micah. We need to talk."

He ducks out from underneath the vehicle. "I thought you were leaving."

I sigh. "It's too late for that."

He frowns. "What are you talking about?"

"I need your help."

He frowns. "What kind of help?"

"Ruth could be in danger. I need to warn her. Do you know where she is?"

"I imagine she's at home. It's about fifteen minutes from here."

"I need the address."

9

Ruth

Before I even opened my eyes, I knew Jack was gone. I reached over to find his side of the bed empty and cold. I sat up and swung my bare feet to the floor, ignoring the painful hollow spot in my chest.

He's gone.

That thought repeated itself, over and over, in my head.

The only man I'd ever met who was strong enough to let me be me. The one man who might not have tried to change me.

I knew he'd be gone, of course. It wasn't a surprise. He'd been perfectly upfront about his plans last night. But still, it hurts. And damn it, I don't want to hurt over this. Over *him*. I just don't.

Still, I can't help the *what if* thoughts that flash through my head.

What if he'd stayed?

What if we'd taken the time to get to know each other?

I knew in my gut that I'd lost an opportunity. Jack was unlike any man I'd ever met. He was so much *more*.

But despite the feeling of *loss*, I know it's best this way. I've had enough failed relationships to last me a lifetime. I don't want another one. Besides, I'd rather be alone than fail again.

I leave the apartment and come straight home to clean up. Even though we used condoms—both times—I still feel a bit sticky. Maybe part of me wants to wash away any reminder of what we shared last night. The sooner I forget about him, the better. I don't want to dwell on lost chances.

After a hot shower, I get dressed and fire up the wood stove to take the chill out of the air. Since I didn't come home last night, the embers in the stove have pretty much died out. I have to start over with fresh kindling and coax the flames to life. While the stove is doing its thing, I put on a pot of coffee and cook some eggs.

I try to keep busy because as soon as I slow down and have a moment to think, my mind replays the events of last night. I remember *everything*—every touch, every taste, every sound. I remember the feel of him inside me, so perfect. The feel of his mouth on mine. I picture him standing behind the bar making me a drink. He looked pretty damn good doing it. I was joking when I asked him if he was looking for a job, but in hindsight I—well, it's pointless now.

He's gone.

I keep reminding myself it's for the best. If he'd stayed, we might have gotten close, and then I'd have the pain of losing him when everything went south. Like it always does.

After I'm done eating and have downed two desperately needed cups of coffee, I wash my dishes, clean up the kitchen, and then walk out to the small red barn that stands at the edge of the clearing. The barn is as old as the cabin, but it's been well maintained.

When we were kids, Micah and I used to play in the barn for hours at a time. It was our sanctuary. Our place to escape. Back then, we got teased a lot by the kids in school. They used a lot of racial slurs, calling us redskins, half breeds, or heathens. They often called me "squaw." I tried desperately to hide how much that hurt.

I step inside and breathe deeply, taking in the lush scent of leather that permeates the building. I don't have any livestock, so there's no feed in here. But there are three stalls—all empty. And, there's a bunkhouse in the rear of the building, with electricity, heat, and running water.

I check the bunkhouse to make sure everything's okay—there are no water leaks, no animal infestations, no birds roosting in the rafters. It is a barn, after all.

Back in his day, my grandfather used to let tavern employees sleep in the bunkhouse if they didn't have anywhere else to go. Now the barn is mostly empty as I use it solely to store my tools.

When I return to the cabin, the wood stove has done its job. It's toasty warm inside. I put a load of clothes in the washer and sit on the sofa to catch up with my reading.

And I try not to think about Jack.

As I'm trying and failing to concentrate on my book, I hear a vehicle coming up my gravel lane. I don't recognize the low, throaty growl. Curious, I abandon my book and walk to the front window to see who's here.

When a black Impala pulls into view, my heart lurches in my chest. *Jack?* It's almost as if my wishful thinking conjured him up.

I step out onto the porch just as he parks in front of the cabin.

When his door opens and he steps out, my breath catches. *Damn.* He's a good-looking man. My pulse kicks into high gear. "What are you doing here?"

He pauses a moment, as if listening, then meets my gaze. "We need to talk."

I step forward and rest my hands on the wooden railing. "About what?"

He takes off his jacket and tosses it into the front passenger seat of his car. Then he closes the driver's door and walks up the wooden steps to meet me on the porch. I note the Glock tucked into a waist holster. I've always suspected he was packing heat.

"There are things you need to know," he says. "I'm not going to sugar coat this, because I know you wouldn't want me to." He pauses, then says, "You might be in danger." He winces. "No, you *are* in danger. And it's my fault."

The butterflies I felt when he arrived quickly turn to stone. "Danger? What are you talking about?"

When the scent of fresh coffee wafts through the screen door, he gives me a wry grin. "Can I trouble you for a cup of coffee first?"

I nod to the door. "Come in."

He follows me inside, closing the door behind him and throwing the dead bolt. I raise a curious brow, but don't say anything.

While I head to the kitchen to pour him some coffee, he scans the small cabin. It's so small, you can pretty much see everything from here.

I hand him his coffee. "All right. Talk." We're standing on opposite sides of the kitchen counter, facing each other.

He takes a sip of his coffee. "Thanks."

"Jack."

He nods to the small dining table behind him. "You might want to sit down for this."

I shake my head as I try to tamp down the warning bells going off in my head. This isn't a social call. He seems tense. "Just tell me."

"Fine." He sets his cup down. "Here it is in a nutshell. I started my military career as a Navy SEAL, eventually becoming a sniper."

I manage not to show any reaction to his announcement.

"I was recruited from the Teams by a private organization—think of them as subcontractors." He chuckles, but the sound is bitter. "Anyway, we mostly do jobs for the CIA. We do a lot of their dirty work. We get our hands dirty so they don't have to."

My stomach knots. "What exactly do you do for them?"

"*Did*," he says emphatically. "I quit six months ago." He pauses a moment, as if reluctant to say more.

"Jack, what the hell—"

"Basically, I was a hitman. My job was to take out designated targets."

"And by *take out*, I assume you mean—"

He nods. "I killed them. Usually from a distance. These were bad people, mind you. Leaders of drug cartels, human traffickers, mass murderers, dictators. You name it. Everything we did was sanctioned by the U.S. government."

I'm still trying to wrap my head around what he just told me. "So, let me get this straight—you *kill* people for a living."

"*Did*. Past tense."

"I see." Not really, but I'm trying to buy time so my brain can catch up. There are a million questions I could ask, but I don't know where to start. I settle on the next one that comes to mind. "Why did you quit?"

He eyes me with a stony expression. "Because it was getting too easy."

"Too easy to kill people? I should hope that would be a problem."

He winces. "You make it sound so tawdry." He gives me a wry grin. "But yeah. Basically, I was finding it too easy to pull the trigger. Too easy to end a person's life. I found myself starting to want something different in life. I realized I wanted to settle down, have a family. As long as I was doing what I was doing, I couldn't have that. I didn't *deserve* to have that."

"So how does this relate to *me*? How does any of this put me in danger?"

Frowning, he looks away, glancing out the kitchen window at the front yard. "The last job I did had some unintended consequences. I was tasked with taking out the boss of a Russian mob organization in New York City. As soon as I did, the guy's younger brother, who was next in line, took over. Immediately, he sent his henchmen out looking for me. Yuri Yevgeny—the new boss—either wants revenge for his brother's death, or he thinks I'll be gunning for him next. Either way, he's put a price on my head."

"And were you going to do that? Kill this man?"

"No, actually. As I said, I'd quit. But Yuri doesn't know that, he doesn't believe it, or he simply doesn't care. The bottom line is—he wants me dead."

Jack picks up his cup and takes a swallow of coffee, wincing as he burns his tongue. He sets his mug down and swipes a hand across his face. "Yevgeny's scouts have been trailing me for the past six months. I was about to leave town this morning when I got wind they're here in Bryce, asking questions."

"How do you know this?"

"Your brother paid me a visit at my motel room this morning. He gave me a heads up."

Now I'm livid. "Someone in the Russian mob spoke to *my brother?*"

Jack has the decency to look guilty. "Yes. I was literally getting ready to pack my car when I learned they were here asking questions. It's only a matter of time before they find out I've been hanging around the tavern. Eventually, they're going to link me with *you.*"

"*Me?* Why me?"

"Because they're not stupid, Ruth. There had to be a reason why I was hanging around this town. It won't take them long to find out *you* are that reason. They only have to ask around town to learn I've been spending every evening in your bar, and well, people talk. I've heard people making comments about me and you."

Suddenly, my knees are weak. I walk around the counter and take a seat at the table before I fall down. "If these mobsters are going to zero in on *me*, that puts my brother in danger, too. My friends. My employees."

Jack nods. "It's possible."

As a wave of nausea sweeps through me, I glare up at Jack, who's leaning against the counter, facing me. The nausea is quickly replaced by anger. "You said you were leaving town this morning!"

He nods. "Honest to God, I was. But I can't leave you to face this alone. I came here to warn you, and I'll stay to protect you—and to stop these thugs in their tracks."

"You're going to fight the mafia, here in Bryce?" I sound skeptical.

He doesn't hesitate. "Yes. I don't have a choice now."

I shake my head. "You're insane."

He steps away from the counter and reaches for my

hand so he can pull me to my feet. His hands cup my shoulders, then slide up to my face. "I'm not going to let anything happen to you."

I gaze into those hard, dark eyes, reading his resolve. I realize I'm looking at someone who's *lethal*. Someone who has a long history of killing people.

"I'm staying," he says. "I'll grab my pack out of my car."

"For how long?"

He shoots me a hard look. "For as long as necessary."

I stand frozen to the spot as Jack walks out the door to retrieve his belongings from his car. He returns a few moments later with a huge rucksack slung over his shoulder. There's no telling what he's got stuffed into that bag. I don't miss the two handguns tucked into his waistband.

"Where should I put my stuff?" he asks.

I point to the bedroom on the left. "That's the spare bedroom."

I follow him as he walks in and sets his bag on the bed. He unzips the bag, pulls out some clothing, and then removes three scary looking rifles, a lethal-looking black knife in a leather sheath, and multiple boxes of ammo.

"What are you doing?" I ask.

"Unpacking."

I eye those rifles with their huge scopes. These aren't like any hunting rifles I've ever seen. These are killing machines.

He carries the boxes of ammo to my closet and stacks them on a shelf above the clothes rod.

"Jack, you can't be serious." I pull my phone out of my back pocket.

He lays his hand over my phone screen. "What are you doing?"

"I'm calling the sheriff."

"No, you're not. Not unless you want him dead."

"What are you talking about?"

"Ruth, you have no idea what these guys are capable of." He pulls one of the handguns from his waistband, pops out the magazine, then checks the chamber. "They won't hesitate to gun down a small-town sheriff. Unless you want your friend killed, keep him out of it. Let me and my buddies handle this."

Feeling queasy, I sit on the mattress as the blood drains from my face, leaving me cold.

10

Jack

Ruth isn't looking so good as I begin making preparations. I check all my weapons and ammo. Then I check all the windows and door locks to make sure the cabin is secured. While I work, Ruth loads another log into the wood stove. She appears to be ignoring me, trying to keep busy, but I know better. I'm sure her mind is racing as she tries to make sense out of what's happening.

"I'm sorry," I say.

She closes the stove door and straightens, her hands going to her hips. "You fucked me knowing this could happen."

Damn. She doesn't pull her punches. "Yeah, I did. I won't apologize for having sex with you, but I am sorry for the rest. The last thing I wanted to do was put you in harm's way."

"And yet, that's exactly what you did." She meets my gaze head-on, unflinching. She doesn't mince words, and I respect that. "I have to leave in an hour," she says, "to open the tavern."

I shake my head. "You're not going to work today, not until this is over."

"I have to. It's *my* bar."

"Ask Tom to handle things for you."

"No! I'm not putting my employees at risk. It's not just Tom, but it's the servers, too, and the kitchen staff. Not to mention my customers. My *friends*."

"I'll call in backup and get some people in your tavern to keep an eye on things."

We both hear it at the same time—the sound of wheels on her gravel drive. I reach behind me for my Glock and check that it's loaded. I also grab my KA-BAR and slip the blade into the sheath strapped to my thigh.

Ruth eyes the gun in my hands. "Stand down, Rambo. It's probably just my brother."

"Maybe," I say as I head to the front window. "But I'm not taking any chances."

She follows me, and we both peer outside as a black SUV stops at the top of the drive, with only its front fender visible. The vehicle is mostly hidden from sight by the trees. Its engine shuts off.

Fuck. "Do you recognize that vehicle?"

"No." Her voice is little more than a whisper. "And none of my friends would stop there. They'd drive up to the cabin."

I figure as much. "Stay back and out of sight, no matter what happens. If I'm not back in ten minutes, call the sheriff. Now, is there another way out of this cabin?"

She points to a door to the right of the kitchen. "You can get out through the laundry room."

"Remember, stay out of sight." I take a step away, then pause to look back at her. "Do you have a gun?"

She nods. "I have two 9mm handguns and a shotgun."

"Get the shotgun. If anyone you don't recognize tries to get inside, shoot him." I don't think it's a coincidence that Micah tells me there's a mobster in town asking questions, and now a stranger shows up at Ruth's house.

Once I'm outside, I move quickly and quietly along the rear of the cabin, then I dart across the yard and into the woods. Using the trees as cover, I make my way toward the lane.

Normally, I'm cool under pressure, but this time, it's not just my safety that's at stake. It's Ruth's. And I'm not going to let these motherfuckers hurt her.

I move through the trees, keeping low as I approach the drive. I'm a bit downhill from the SUV, which gives me an advantage because the intruder is undoubtedly focused on the cabin, looking either for me or for Ruth. I wouldn't put it past these assholes to target her instead of coming at me head-on.

I slip through the trees, silent as air, and come up behind the SUV. The perp is standing outside the vehicle, a rifle trained on the cabin as if he's just waiting for a target. He's dressed head to toe in black, his face covered as well. I can see the Yevgeny organization's signature tattoos covering his neck. He might as well be sporting a neon sign.

The guy's phone vibrates, and he thumbs the screen. "*Da?*"

I listen as he speaks Russian to someone on the line. "*YA nashel yego.*" I found him. "*On s zhenshchinoy.*" He's with a woman. A moment later, the guy says, "*Konechno, ya ub'yu ikh oboikh.*" *Sure, I'll kill them both.*

That's good enough for me.

This needs to be quick and quiet. I tuck my Glock back into my holster and pull out my KA-BAR. Silently, I sneak up behind him as he peers through his rifle's scope. He's so focused on finding a target, he doesn't hear me. A heartbeat later, I'm on him, slicing clean through his carotid. He drops to the ground like a stone, blood gurgling in his throat.

Not a shot fired.

After ensuring he's no longer a threat, I drag him to the back of his vehicle and deposit him inside. I dig through his pockets and locate his phone and his wallet. He has a New York driver's license. I unlock his phone using his own face, then remove the security settings to keep it unlocked so I can go through it later.

After driving the SUV through the clearing and parking it beside the barn, I walk up to the cabin's front door. "Ruth, it's me!" I hope she's not trigger-happy. "You can stand down now."

The front door opens and Ruth peers outside, her gaze sweeping the clearing in front of her home, eyes sharp and assessing. "Where is he?"

"He's in the back of his SUV."

"Is he—"

"Dead? Yes."

"Are you sure—"

"Am I sure he's dead? Yes."

"No, I meant are you *sure* he's with the mafia? That he came here to kill you?"

I pull a black leather wallet from my jacket pocket and flash her the New York state driver's license. "He's one of Yevgeny's men. I heard him talking to them on the phone—in Russian. His handlers told him to kill both of us. So, yes, I'm sure." I nod toward the barn. "I'll park the SUV in the barn until I can dispose of it."

Ruth pales as she stares at me. "Shouldn't we call the sheriff's office?"

"And tell them what? That I just slit the throat of a tourist from the Big Apple?" I shake my head. "No, thanks."

"You said he was a scout. Are you implying there will be more?"

A harsh laugh escapes me. "More? You can count on it. Plenty more, including Yevgeny himself. Or at least I hope so. This ends with him." I watch the blood drain from Ruth's face as this news sinks in. "This isn't over.

Far from it. We're just getting started."

"I've got to warn the others," she says. "My brother, my employees. I need to warn Chris and my friends."

"Chris is the sheriff?"

She nods and pulls out her phone.

I lay a hand on it, stopping her from making the call. "You can't get anyone else involved—that will only put their lives at risk. Ruth, you need to leave town until this is resolved. Is there somewhere you can go? Somewhere you'll be safe?"

She shakes her head. "I'm not leaving my family and friends to deal with this."

"It's not safe—"

"If it's not safe for me, it's not safe for them either. I'm staying."

I'm so frustrated I could—oh, hell, I don't know what I could do. It's not like I can give her an ultimatum. It wouldn't work. Ruth's not going to budge, and I won't force her. I probably couldn't even if I tried. I've never met such a strong-willed woman in my life. "Look, I'll make some calls and get us some help," I tell her. "In the meanwhile, let's move this SUV into the barn to get it out of sight."

Ruth follows me outside and slides open the wide

barn door so I can drive the vehicle inside. After stepping out of the SUV, I pull a small, high-powered flashlight out of my pocket and get down on my knees so I can scan the underside of the carriage.

"What are you looking for?" she asks, following me as I make my way around the vehicle.

"A tracker." I finally locate one in the rear left wheel well. "Damn it." I pull it off, drop it on the ground, and crush it with my bootheel. Of course, it's too little, too late. Yevgeny already knows the last known location of the vehicle. It's only a matter of time before his men show up here.

I pop the rear door to deal with the body lying in the back. "Can I use this?" I ask, pointing at a blue plastic tarp lying on the ground.

Ruth shrugs. "Sure."

"Have you got a spare rope?" I ask.

"I'll find one." She returns a moment later with a nylon rope, which I use to secure the tarp around the body.

"Have you seen a lot of dead bodies?" I ask.

"This would be my first." Remarkably, she maintains her composure as her gaze locks on the body as I close the rear hatch door. "We can't just leave him here. The body—"

"Don't worry. It'll be gone by tonight."

"Gone where?"

"Somewhere suitable. It's best you don't know."

Ruth shakes her head. "I can't believe we're having this discussion."

"Welcome to my world. Well, my previous world."

"And then what?" she asks. "Who will come after you next?"

I shrug. It's a good question—one I've been trying to answer myself. "You probably don't want to know."

* * *

After closing up the barn, we return to the cabin. Ruth disappears into her bedroom, where she remains until around two that afternoon. When she finally comes out of hiding, she's dressed in a pair of worn blue jeans and a red flannel plaid shirt over a white tank top. Her hair is neatly braided, and she's wearing feather earrings and a turquoise necklace. *Damn. She's stunning.*

"Where do you think you're going?" I ask, although I'm pretty sure I already know the answer.

"To work." She grabs her wallet and keys off the kitchen counter.

I step in front of her, cutting her off. "Ruth, no. You can't. Ask Tom to take over for you."

"I told you, I'm not going to hide out here while my employees might be in harm's way." She reaches around to pat the small of her back, where undoubtedly she's carrying a handgun. "I won't be without protection."

I have to fight the urge to roll my eyes. One woman pitted against mobsters who won't hesitate to gun her down.

"That's right," I say. "You won't be without protection because I'm coming with you." When she looks like she's about to argue with me, I cut her off. "It's not up for discussion. I'm coming."

11

Ruth

As I drive to town, Jack follows me in his Impala. We park in the rear lot, out of sight of passersby who might be driving along Main Street. Tom's truck is already here, parked in his reserved spot behind the building. That doesn't surprise me. He's almost always early. When we walk inside, I find Tom restocking the rack of beer mugs. He turns to me, his coolly assessing gaze going from me to Jack.

"Hiya, Tom," Jack says to my assistant manager.

"Jack," Tom says, his tone neutral as he tries to suss out the situation.

Jack checks his watch. "You might as well put me to work, Ruth. The place won't open for another half hour. What can I do?"

"I could use some help in the storage room," I say. "We need to restock the bar."

Jack motions down the back hallway. "Lead the way, boss."

I can tell by the guarded expression on Tom's face that he wants a word. "Go ahead, Jack. I'll be right there."

Jack's gaze transfers from me to Tom. "Sure thing."

When Jack is out of sight, Tom raises a questioning eyebrow. "I know it's none of my business," he begins, "but—"

"Actually, it *is* your business. You need to know—there might be some unsavory people arriving in town before long, and they might come here looking for Jack."

"Unsavory people?"

"It's a long story, but suffice it to say that Jack's made some serious enemies in New York City. They might come here looking for him."

"*Unsavory people?*" he repeats. "That means what, exactly?"

I wince. "Members of an organized crime syndicate."

Tom's pale blue eyes widen. "You mean mafia?" His voice rises. "Your boyfriend pissed off the *mafia?*"

"He's not my boyfriend," I hiss. "Keep your voice down. But, yes, he pissed off the Russian mafia. So, be alert. Keep your eyes and ears open."

"Have you told Chris?"

"Not exactly."

"Why the hell not?"

"Jack doesn't want the police involved. He says it's too dangerous for them."

"Holy crap, Ruth. You need to send this guy packing."

"I'm afraid it's too late for that." I glance down the hallway toward the storage room. "I'll be back."

I join Jack in the storage room, where he's standing idle in the center of the room with his arms crossed over his chest.

"Are you two done talking about me behind my back?" he asks, trying hard not to smile.

"For the time being, yes. But don't be surprised if it happens again."

He walks past me and closes the door, shutting us in together, before pulling me into his arms. "I haven't had a chance to tell you, but last night was amazing."

He leans in and kisses me, tentatively at first, as if he's not sure of my reaction.

I push him back, although it's only half-heartedly. "Don't even try. After everything that's going on, you don't get to act like nothing's wrong."

He frowns. "I'm not. I told you I was sorry, Ruth." His expression flattens. "I never meant to stay in town this long. I kept telling myself I'd leave the next morning, but when the time came, I couldn't bring myself to do it." He leans in and gives me a surprisingly tender kiss. "I didn't want to leave you."

I scoff. "You hardly know me."

He gives me a small smile. "I know enough."

There's an undeniable pull between us, a sexual tug at the very least. Maybe even an emotional one, if I'm being honest with myself. At least I feel it. I can't vouch for what he's feeling. I reach up and stroke his cheek, running my thumb along a tanned strip of skin just above his beard. He closes his eyes, reminding me of a cat relishing affection.

"What's going to happen now?" I ask. "I need to know."

He opens his eyes and frowns, the tender moment obviously over. "When they get here, I'll try to lure them away, to a remote location where we can end this thing once and for all. My guys are coming. I'll have backup. And as for you—"

"Don't even suggest it. I'm not running."

Jack smiles. "You're such a mama bear. That's one of the things I love about you. You don't pull your punches, and you take no prisoners."

All I heard was *love about you*. And now there's a roaring in my ears.

"Ruth!" Tom yells. "It's nearly three o'clock. Do you want me to unlock the doors?"

"Yeah, go ahead," I yell back. "I'll be right there!"

Jack frowns as I start to move to the door. "Ruth—"

I point at a half dozen cases of beer bottles on the floor. "You want to be helpful? Carry those to the bar." And then I open the door and walk out, all the while ignoring the pain in my chest.

That's one of the things I love about you.

* * *

While Tom's taking care of the rear entrance, I go to the front door, switch on the neon OPEN sign, and unlock the door. As usual, there's a short line of customers waiting outside. I open the door and hold it as our first few customers come in. I greet some familiar faces and scrutinize anyone I don't recognize.

Chrissy and Jess arrive through the back door, along with Casey. The kitchen staff is poised and ready for orders. Tom and I take our customary places behind the bar.

After delivering the cases of beer, as I'd requested, Jack takes his usual seat at the far end of the bar. I watch him out of the corner of my eye and notice that he's observing everyone who walks in.

I keep thinking about that black SUV parked in my barn. More specifically, I keep thinking about the dead body lying in the back of it. Gruesome questions come to mind, like how long before *rigor mortis* sets in? Or, how long before there's a noticeable odor?

I offer Jack a beer, but he declines, telling me he's essentially on duty and therefore can't drink. So I bring him a Coke instead, setting it on the counter in front of him. "Surely a soft drink won't kill you. And, since we missed lunch, I ordered you a burger and fries. Your food will be out in a minute."

He presses his hand to his chest. "A woman after my own heart. Thanks," he says, keeping one eye on the door. "If anyone you don't recognize walks in, give me a heads-up."

Just as he says that, the front door opens, and his attention is diverted to a group of college-aged guys walking in, clearly hikers. Once he's satisfied they're no threat, his gaze returns to me. "If something happens, I want you to lock yourself in your office, okay?" Before I can even respond, he says, "Promise me, Ruth. No Wonder Woman heroics. You let me handle it."

My smile quickly fades when I think of the real potential for violence in my tavern. There are a lot of people in here who could get hurt. The obvious solution—the *only* solution—is for me to close the bar.

I'm pouring a draft beer for a customer when two unfamiliar men walk in through the back hallway. Both are tall, dressed in black, and look overly vigilant. One has brown hair and brown eyes, the other blond with blue eyes.

When they both pause to scan the room, warning bells go off in my head, and my heart starts pounding. Immediately, I look to Jack, to signal to him that these guys may be a problem, but it's unnecessary. He's already on his feet, his gaze glued to the two men.

One of the newcomers elbows his companion as he

nods toward Jack. "There he is," he says in a heavily-accented voice. He's definitely not from around here. I don't speak Russian, but if I had to guess, I'd say we have a match.

I reach behind me for the handgun tucked into my waistband.

"Ruth." Jack's voice is clipped, his tone sharp.

When I glance at him, he shakes his head. *No.*

As Jack approaches the two men, they break into big grins. He hugs each one, smacking them on their backs.

"You are a sight for sore eyes, my friend," says the big blond, the one with the accent.

The other one shakes Jack's hand. "Good to see you're still in one piece, buddy." *An American accent.*

"This way," Jack says to the two men. He catches my gaze and nods down the hallway toward my office, gesturing for me to join them.

I follow them into my office, and Jack closes the door behind us.

"Ruth, these are my friends." He nods to the one with brown hair. "Mike Roman." He nods to the blond. "Aleksa Vukovich."

"It is a pleasure to make your acquaintance, ma'am," the blond says as he offers me his hand. He grips mine firmly as we shake. To Jack, he says, "This must be the pretty scenery, yes?"

Jack lightly punches the blond man's broad shoulder. "Knock it off, Lexi." To me, he says, "By the way, in case you're wondering, Aleksa is Serbian, not Russian."

"I did wonder," I say.

"Don't worry," the blond—Aleksa—says. "I'm one of the good guys."

"Where's the body?" the other man asks Jack. All business, he gets right to the point.

"In an SUV parked in Ruth's barn. We need to dispose of them tonight—both the body and the vehicle."

The one named Mike Roman nods. "Lexi and I will take care of it."

Jack nods to his friend. "Thanks." Then he looks at me. "If it's okay with you, Ruth, we'll all hole up at your place for the time being. It's out of the way and easily defensible. Just tell your friends and your brother to keep away. We don't want to shoot any of them by mistake."

"Diego and Lenny will be here by morning," Mike says. "With the five of us, we'll be able to hold our ground."

"You're going to turn my home into a war zone?" I ask.

Jack winces. "Sorry, but yes. It's the safest place to end this." Then he addresses his friends. "I'm sure Yevgeny's men are on the way since their scout hasn't checked in for several hours now."

"Do you think the big man himself will come?" Aleksa asks.

"You mean Yuri?" Jack nods. "I'm counting on it."

"This bar is a security nightmare," Mike says to Jack. "Two entrances? Anyone can walk in, and if there's trouble, there's going to be significant collateral damage. It'll be unavoidable."

Jack turns his attention to me.

"All right," I say, knowing there's no other option. "I'll close the bar until this is over."

"I'm sorry, Ruth," Jack says.

"So you keep saying."

12

Jack

I feel like shit for bringing all this down on Ruth's head, for disrupting her life, her business. Putting her friends at risk. She has a quiet word with Tom and the rest of her staff as she notifies them that she's closing the bar. I watch her walk to the jukebox and shut it off. Everyone immediately quiets down and looks at Ruth.

"Hey, folks," she says, smiling apologetically. "I'm afraid I'm going to have to shut down early this evening."

There's a loud, collective groan of disappointment.

"I'm offering everyone one last drink, on the house," she says, which results in a smattering of cheer. "And all your tabs and orders today are comped." That earns her an even stronger response, with a few hoots and hollers thrown in.

Oh, great. Not only am I disrupting her life, but I'm costing her money as well. I walk up beside her. "I'll reimburse you for your losses."

She glances at me, her expression hard to read, and shakes her head. "Don't bother."

Ouch.

After a chaotic run of last drinks, Tom turns off the OPEN sign and holds the front door while the customers file out. Mike monitors the back door to make sure no undesirables sneak in.

Once everyone's out, Tom turns off all the lights as Ruth locks the front door.

"I need to stop at the diner and the grocery store," Ruth says. "We'll need extra supplies at the cabin, and I need to warn my friends."

I want to tell her no, that it's a bad idea. That we need to get back to her place and set up our defenses before it gets dark, but the expression on her face tells me otherwise. "Ruth—"

"If you're worried, you can go back to the cabin without me," she says. "I'll be along shortly."

"I'm staying with you."

She shrugs. "Suit yourself."

We walk around the side of the building to the front sidewalk. The diner is right next door. This close to the dinner rush, the place is packed.

Jenny spots us the moment we walk in and waves. "Have a seat, guys. Anywhere you want."

"Wait here," Ruth says to me. Then she flags down Jenny, and the two of them make their way down the hall that leads to the restrooms.

As Ruth talks, Jenny's dark eyes widen, her gaze flickering over to me where I'm standing at the entrance. Jenny says something to Ruth, and Ruth answers. My ears are definitely burning.

I'm still stationed by the door, scanning the street, when Ruth walks past me and out onto the sidewalk. "What did you say to her?" I ask as I fall in step beside her.

I can tell she's still pissed at me. She heads next door to the grocery store, which is owned by another of her friends. Before she can step inside, I grab her arm. "What did you tell her?"

"The truth." She sounds exasperated. "That you've attracted some dangerous people to Bryce. That she needs to be vigilant, and that if she spots *anything* suspicious, she needs to call the sheriff's office."

Ruth pulls out of my grasp and walks into Emerson's Grocery Store. I follow her inside.

A woman with long, curly brown hair pulled back in a ponytail is standing behind the sales counter. The woman's face lights up when she spots Ruth.

"Ruth, hi!" she says. "How's it going?" Her curious gaze transfers to me.

"Hi, Maggie," Ruth says.

Her friend is eyeing me curiously. Ruth introduces us. "This is my friend Maggie. Maggie, this is Jack."

Maggie smiles. "It's nice to meet you, officially."

Ruth grabs a shopping cart and heads for the refrigerated cases. I take the cart from her. "I'll push. You grab supplies."

Ruth is definitely preparing for a siege because she buys several of everything—four dozen eggs, four loaves of bread.

When we pass the snack aisle, I grab several bags of potato chips and some pretzels. Ruth watches, but doesn't say anything. In the beverage aisle, she grabs two cases of Fat Tire and two cases of Coke. Once the cart is loaded up, we head for the checkout. I grab a handful of candy bars and put them on the counter. "You're worse than a kid," Ruth says, rolling her eyes. As Maggie rings up our purchases, she bites her lip. "Are you feeding a small army?" she asks Ruth. "Your total is two-hundred and ten dollars."

Before Ruth can retrieve her wallet from her back pocket, I grab mine and fish out enough cash to pay the bill. "Here, I've got it." I hand Maggie the money.

When we're done, I head out a back door, which opens out into the rear parking lot, close to our vehicles. I push the cart to Ruth's Jeep, and after she opens the back, we load six sacks of groceries into the vehicle, along with the beer and pop.

She closes the back door. "That was nice of you to pay for the groceries. Thanks."

"It's the least I can do, since they're *my* friends."

"Well, thanks. I appreciate it. I guess I'll see you back at the cabin." She gets in her Jeep and drives away.

I follow her in my car. Mike and Aleksa, who waited

for us, take up the rear in their black SUV.

The entire drive to the cabin, Ruth's on the phone with someone. My guess is she's talking to her brother. I sure hope she's not calling the sheriff. He's more than just law enforcement to her—he's a friend. And she might be compelled to give her friend a heads-up. The problem is, we don't need local law enforcement getting caught in the crossfire.

My guys and I can handle this, but if the local small-town cops got involved, they'd be walking blind into a potential blood bath.

13

Ruth

When we arrive at my place, I park in my usual spot near the front porch. Jack pulls up beside me. His two friends park their SUV on the far side of the barn, out of sight. While we carry in the groceries, Jack's friends slip into the barn. I imagine they're making plans to dispose of the body. I don't even want to think about how and where they're going to do that.

I feel like I'm living an episode of *Law and Order*,

or maybe it's more like *The Equalizer*. Surely, this kind of thing doesn't happen in the real world. I can't help thinking I'm going to end up a fugitive from the law, or at least a person of interest, when this is all over. Or maybe even an accessory to a crime. But it was self-defense, right? What Jack did—killing an armed mafia thug who was pointing a rifle at my house. Who'd come here with the intention of killing Jack, and perhaps me along with him.

We carry the groceries into the cabin, and I immediately start unpacking the haul. I picked up the basics—milk, eggs, bread, beef, cheese, beer, soft drinks, and coffee. Plenty of coffee. Some fresh fruits, veggies, and lettuce. Toilet paper and paper towels. I even bought extra supplies to stock the bunkhouse as well. There's no telling how long we might find ourselves barricaded here.

"Your friends can stay in the bunkhouse," I say. "In the barn. It's comfortable. There's a small kitchen and a bathroom. It has electricity, heat, and running water."

Jack chuckles. "Thanks. I'll let them know."

"Feel free to join them." I'm still mad at him for bringing this trouble to my town—hell, to my door. I'm also feeling a bit unsettled because he was supposed to be gone by now, out of my life. My one-night stand is still here the next day. It wasn't supposed to go like that.

Jack's smile fades. "Look, I know you're pissed at me, and you have good reason to be. But I'm not staying in the bunkhouse. I'm staying in the cabin *with you*."

I shove a package of paper towels into the cupboard. "I don't need you to babysit me."

"I don't care what you call it, but I'm sticking by your side." He grabs the four cartons of eggs off the counter and puts them in the refrigerator. "Who did you call on the drive here? I saw you on your phone."

"I made two calls. One to my friend Hannah, at The Wilderness Lodge, to give her a heads-up. The other call was to my brother."

"Fair enough. But the fewer people who know what's about to happen, the better."

"Better for them, or for you?" I ask, failing to keep the sharp tone from my voice.

"For them," he says with a sigh, as if he's tired of defending himself. "So, am I still in the spare bedroom? I'm guessing your bed is not an option."

"You think?"

He nods. "Fair enough. At least it's better than the sofa or the barn. But if you change your mind about sharing your bed—"

Growling, I grab a kitchen towel, ball it up, and lob it at his head.

He catches it effortlessly and turns away so I can't see him grinning.

* * *

Later that evening, when I'm seated at the desk in my bedroom finishing up cleaning my shotgun and two handguns, there's a knock on my door. "Come in."

Jack opens the door and steps inside, his hands going to his hips as he observes my preparations. "Let's hope you won't need any of those."

I shrug. "What do you want?"

He winces. "Still pissed, I see." When I don't bother to reply, he adds, "I just wanted to let you know that Mike and Aleksa just left to take care of business."

"You mean they're dumping the dead body."

"Yeah."

"Where?" Even though I ask, I'm not sure I want to know. Are they dumping the body in a river, where a fisherman might encounter it? In a ravine, where hikers could stumble across it and be traumatized? Or, are they burying it deep somewhere off the beaten path where no one will ever find it? That last one would be my choice.

"The less you know, the better," he says. "If this goes south, you can honestly claim you have no knowledge of what's going on."

He crosses my bedroom and closes the curtains hanging in front of the two windows. "You should keep your curtains closed and turn off your lights as soon as possible. It'll make it much harder for someone to see inside the cabin and monitor your whereabouts."

"You have this all figured out, don't you?"

"I've been dealing with situations like this for a long time."

I load a full magazine into my 9mm and stash it in the middle drawer of my nightstand. I put the other handgun in a box on the top shelf in my closet, along with the shotgun. Finally, I switch off the lamp beside the bed. "Happy now?"

He chuckles. "Far from it."

"Too bad." I walk past him and out the door.

"Where are you going?" he asks as he follows me out.

"To load the wood stove for the night and get ready for bed."

"I already took care of the stove," he says.

"Fine." So I head for the bathroom instead.

"Sleep in your clothes tonight," he says through the closed bathroom door. "Be ready to move at a moment's notice."

After cleaning up, I open the bathroom door, surprised to see he's waiting there, leaning against the wall. The rest of the cabin is dark. All the lights are off, and the curtains are drawn.

"Can I help you?" I ask.

Jack exhales heavily. "Ruth, I really am sorry."

My throat tightens. I hate being mad at him, but I don't know how to shake this. I don't like feeling out of control. I hate the unknown. I hate worrying about Micah and my friends. "So you keep saying." I want to say it's okay, that I understand, but the words die in my throat.

When I pass him on the way to my bedroom, he grasps my shoulders and maneuvers me so that my back is flush against the wall.

His touch is light, but it's enough to keep me there because my traitorous body likes it. I think back to last night and early this morning, to sharing a bed with him. *Was it really only this morning?* It seems like it was a lifetime ago. I want that again, so badly. And I hate myself for it. I don't want to like him. I don't want to *want* him.

My heart starts pounding and my belly clenches in anticipation. "What are you doing, Jack?" I'm trying desperately to hold onto my resentment, but the truth is, it's slipping away.

He leans close, his hands framing my face. I gaze into a pair of dark eyes, lit with an intensity that steals my breath. "I'm sorry," he says again. His gaze drops to my lips, and I know he's thinking of kissing me.

When I thought he was leaving the next day, I was okay with having sex. But now everything has changed. He's not leaving—at least not anytime soon. And that changes everything. A one-night stand I could deal with, but anything more than that—no. I'm not going through that again.

I press my hand to his chest. "We need to talk, Jack. Or, rather *you* do. I want to know what's going on. *All of it.*"

He's silent for a moment, as if warring with himself, trying to decide what he can tell me, if anything. Then, he nods through my open bedroom door at my bed. "All right. Sit."

I take a seat on my bed as he starts pacing.

"Yuri's outfit has been dogging me since I left the organization. Somehow they seem to be just a few steps behind me. I've made it a point to keep moving since I retired. I've never spent more than a day in one location. I slept in my car more often than not. I ate drive-thru and gas station food. I paid to take showers in truck stops. As long as I kept moving, I was fine. They couldn't catch up to me. But I made a mistake by staying in Bryce too long."

"How are they tracking you?"

Jack shakes his head. "There has to be a mole in my old organization. The only ones who know my whereabouts are *my guys*—my former team members. They've been monitoring my location."

"You mean Mike and Aleksa?"

"They're not the moles," he says, shaking his head adamantly. "I'd stake my life on it."

"It sounds like you already are."

He's still shaking his head. "Mike and I served together in the SEAL Teams. He's like a brother to me. Same for Lexi."

"Then who else is there?"

"There are two other guys—Diego and Lenny. They're on their way."

My eyes widen. "So, your potential mole is coming here?"

He nods. "Mike and I thought this would be the best way to identify the mole—if we had him right under our noses and could set a trap for him."

"So, now what?"

He chuckles bitterly. "Now I take out Yuri Yevgeny. Ironically, I have to do the one thing I hadn't planned on doing. But he's forced my hand. This won't stop until one of us is dead—it's either him or me."

"Can you do that? Take this guy out? I mean, if he comes with an army of his own?"

Jack nods. "With the five of us standing together, Yuri and his henchmen don't stand a chance." He says that with utter confidence, although there's no joy or satisfaction in his voice. It's clear he doesn't want to do this. That he's being forced into it.

His jaw tightens. "My only other option is to leave the country and cut all ties to my former teammates, to everyone. If the mole doesn't know where I am, then Yuri won't be able to trace me. Not without the insider information he's getting now."

"No." The thought of Jack banishing himself, friendless, is unacceptable. "You can't keep running."

"Would you please reconsider leaving town until this is over?" he asks. "Your brother could take you somewhere. Or I can ask Mike to do it."

I turn to face him. "Sorry, no. I'm not the running type."

He smiles. "Yeah, I kind of figured that. I guess that's why I'm so attracted to you." He tucks a loose strand of hair behind my ear. "You have an inner strength I find irresistible."

The way he's looking at me makes my breath catch. His gaze is locked on mine, as if he's searching for something. "I wish things were different," he says.

I nod. "Me, too." I wish I weren't afraid of trying again and that I was willing to take a chance.

When his phone chimes with an incoming text message, Jack checks the screen. "It's from Mike. They found a place to dump the body and the vehicle."

"Where?"

"He didn't say, although I take it the location isn't close by because he says they won't make it back before the wee hours. We're on our own for the next four or five hours." He glances at his watch. "It's getting late. You should try to get some sleep. The next twenty-four hours are going to be hairy."

"What about you?"

He shrugs. "I'm on guard duty until the guys return.

You go to bed."

"I can wait up with you."

Jack shakes his head. "I'd rather you didn't. You're going to need rest, sleep if you can get it." He gets up and walks to my door, turning just to say, "Goodnight, Ruth. I'll be right here if you need me."

And then he's gone, closing the door behind him and leaving me alone with my thoughts. I should be focused on what might happen, but instead my head keeps replaying Jack's words to me.

I'm sorry.

He's apologized several times for bringing his troubles into my life, and I believe he's sincere. If I'm being honest with myself, the truth is I'm not mad at him. I'm just scared. I'm afraid to risk my peace, and my heart, taking a chance on another guy.

But if there was ever a guy worth taking a chance on, it would have to be Jack Merchant.

14

Jack

I meant it when I told Ruth the next twenty-four hours were going to be hairy. I can predict exactly what's going to happen. Mike and Lexi will return to the cabin. Diego and Lenny will show up shortly after, around dawn. And sometime tomorrow evening, after darkness falls, the Yevgeny crowd will arrive with the intention of killing me, as well as anyone with me. That puts not only my guys at risk, but Ruth as well.

I'd give anything to be able to talk my team into leaving while there's still time, but I know my pleas will fall on deaf ears. Just as Ruth refuses to leave town. Stubborn folks, all of them. But I guess I can't blame them as I'd do the same for any of them.

It's going to be a long night, so I put on a pot of coffee. All of the interior lights are off. The windows and doors are locked. The curtains are drawn, except for those hanging in the front living room window. Those are wide open, giving me a wide-angle view of the front of the cabin. From my vantage point in the living room, I'll be able to see any vehicles coming up the drive. I can also spot anyone trying to sneak up to the front of the cabin.

Earlier this evening, I'd gone out to the barn to scout around and was gratified to find a second story loft at the east end of the structure, with a small window that provides the perfect line of sight across the clearing to the lane. From there, any one of us could hunker down with a sniper rifle and provide some serious support. It'll have to be Mike, as next to me, he's our best sharpshooter. I can't do it because I need to stay close to Ruth. Diego would be my next choice, but I don't want him up there in the sniper's box. I want him on the ground where I can keep an eye on him. He and Lenny are our two possible snitches.

Diego Ramirez served in the US Marine Corps for ten years. Lenny Maxwell was an Army Green Beret with just as much experience. I've known Lenny for years. Diego is new to the group. He joined just eighteen months ago. I suspect one of them has been selling intel on me to Yevgeny. The alternatives are Mike and Aleksa, which I just can't accept. If I'm wrong, though, it could get me killed. It could get all of us killed. Including Ruth.

I haven't completely given up hope that I can talk Ruth into leaving town, or at least leaving the cabin. Maybe she'd consider staying with her friends at The Lodge for a few days, or maybe with her brother. I'll try talking some sense into her in the morning.

I'm on my second cup of strong, black coffee when I hear Ruth's bedroom door open. She walks into the living room, barefoot and dressed in gray flannel lounge pants and a form-fitting white tank top that reveals her muscular arms and hugs her firm breasts. Her skin is a gorgeous shade of light brown.

My dick stirs at the sight of her, undoubtedly remembering what we did together last night, and again early this morning.

"I can't sleep," she says as she sits on the arm of the sofa, just feet away from me. She peers out the window at the moonlit clearing. "Everything quiet out there?"

"The calm before the storm, yeah. Hey, I made coffee." I nod toward the kitchen.

She smiles but shakes her head. "I came to get an update."

"Mike and Lexi are on their way back. ETA one hour."

"They succeeded in doing what they set out to do?"

I nod. "Mission accomplished." When she frowns, I remind her that the guy I offed had orders to kill *both* of us. "So they know you're here. You're a target now. That's why I want you to leave. It's too late for me to move the party elsewhere. This property is the last known location for the scout. They're going to come here regardless of where I am."

She runs her hands up and down her bare arms. "This feels so unreal."

"I assure you it's real. It's going to get really real when the bullets start flying." I turn to look her in the eye. "When Yevgeny's men arrive, I want you holed up in the bathroom. It's the safest room in the cabin—interior with no windows. I want you to lock yourself in there and stay put until the coast is clear. Take your handgun and shotgun with you."

"This isn't anything new for you, is it?" she asks. "A life and death situation, I mean. You're used to it."

"I spent the past two decades of my life right in the middle of shit like this."

She's quiet a moment. Finally, she says, "I owe you an apology, Jack, for being so bitchy to you. I was angry—upset—but that's no excuse."

"There's no need to apologize. I understand."

"It's just that I thought you were leaving. When I agreed to have sex with you—hell, I'm the one who initiated it—I did it thinking you were *leaving*."

"Are you saying you wouldn't have slept with me if you knew I was going to hang around?" That's a new one. In my experience, women bitch at guys for leaving.

"Yes." She gets up to check the wood stove, stirs the embers, and adds another log. "It wasn't so complicated when I thought you weren't staying. Now, well, everything's changed."

I figure I might as well put my cards on the table. "Ruth, I slept with you because I wanted you. I like you, a lot. It wasn't just a one-night stand for me."

She smiles. "I know." She sighs. "To be honest, I wanted you, too. Badly."

"But?"

"But, I'm not looking for a relationship. You weren't supposed to still be here."

I bite back a chuckle. "Well, the situation changed on me. My plans changed." I get up and walk to the kitchen to refill my cup. "Why are you so dead set against a relationship?"

"I was married once, and it ended badly. A few years later, against my better judgment, I tried again, but it ended just as badly. Fortunately, that time, I wasn't stupid enough to marry him."

"Maybe you just haven't met the right guy." I smile. "Maybe the third time's the charm."

"I'm not holding my breath." She gazes out the window at the front yard cloaked in darkness and shadows. "Apparently, and I'm quoting here," she says, "I'm too strong-willed. I'm difficult. I'm a ballbuster."

I can't help laughing. "Who said this? Your husband?"

"Pretty much every man I've ever dated."

"Then you're dating the wrong men. They were intimidated by you, Ruth. They resented your strength. You threatened their sense of power or dominance. You challenged their authority. But you know, some of us actually admire strong women. I, for one, do."

"I don't need a man," she says. "I do just fine on my own. I have a successful business, I own my own home, and I can deal with my own spiders."

I smile at that last bit. "I know you don't *need* a man, but maybe it's okay to want one. Maybe there's room in your life for one who respects your independence and your boundaries."

She gives me a wry glance. "Don't talk to me of boundaries, pal."

"Okay, point taken. But still."

When she opens her mouth to reply, the sound of tires approaching on the gravel diverts our attention to the front window.

I reach for my rifle as I wait to get a look at the vehicle. When I see the make and model of the black SUV with Kansas license plates, I stand down. "It's okay. It's just Mike and Lexi." I check my watch. "They made good time getting back."

Lexi parks the SUV across the yard from the cabin, perpendicular to the tree line to create a barrier between the lane and the barn.

I meet them at the door. "How'd it go?"

"It's done," Mike says as he walks into the cabin. "It'll be a long time before anyone finds anything, if ever. And there sure won't be any physical evidence left at that point."

I nod. "Good."

"Why don't you get some sleep?" Mike asks me. "I'll take over watch duty." He looks at Ruth. "You, too, ma'am. You should try to get some sleep. You're going to need it."

Ruth retreats to her bedroom, closing the door behind her.

"Anything to report?" Lexi asks me.

"No," I say. "It's been quiet. I don't think they'll show up before nightfall."

"We'll be ready," Mike says. "We can deploy motion sensors around the property in the morning. They won't be able to sneak up on us."

Standing by the front window, I point up at the window on the second story of the barn, overlooking the yard. "That's our best vantage point for a sharpshooter."

Mike nods. "I'll do it." He lays his hand on my shoulder. "Go get some sleep. Lexi and I will split up watch duty for the next few hours."

"Just don't shoot Diego and Lenny when they arrive," I say, chuckling. "We need all the help we can get."

I leave everything in Mike and Lexi's hands, hit the

john, brush my teeth, and then walk into the guest bedroom. It's pretty barebones, but comfortable.

I crash on the mattress, lying on my back. Thanks to all the caffeine, I'm a bit buzzed. I don't think I could sleep even if I weren't. Ruth's words keep replaying in my head. It infuriates me that men have criticized her for being too strong. I see a strong woman as an asset, and men who don't are weak and easily intimidated.

At some point, I must have dozed off, because the next thing I know, sunrise is filtering through the curtains, and I hear quiet voices coming from the living room. I check the time—it's seven already.

I leave the bedroom and find Diego and Lenny in the kitchen, drinking coffee. "Hey, guys. Thanks for coming."

Diego approaches first, his hand out. "Long time, no see, pal," he says, grabbing me by the hand and pulling me into a quick embrace.

"Good to see you, too, Diego."

Lenny steps forward, offering me a lopsided grin as he pulls me in for a bear hug. "I've missed you, man. How about you come back to the team after this is over? It's not the same without you."

I have to admit, the thought of all five of us together again feels good. But I'm not going back. I left that life for a reason, a *good* reason. I want to put down roots. I want a family. I want to deserve that. "Thanks for coming, guys. Thanks to all of you. I really appreciate the help. I can't do this alone."

Ruth's bedroom door opens, and she walks out dressed in jeans and a burgundy sweatshirt with a *Ruth's Tavern* logo on it. She pauses as she scans the new arrivals.

"Guys, this is Ruth," I say. "This is her cabin. Ruth, allow me to introduce you to Lenny and Diego, two of my former teammates."

Ruth shakes their hands. "Welcome. Now, how about some breakfast?"

15

Ruth

This must be what it's like to be a college dormitory room mother. My small cabin is bursting at the seams with five men who are all larger than life. I offer to make breakfast, and find myself going through nearly two dozen eggs, a pound of bacon, and an entire loaf of bread. I thought I was doing good to stock up on the necessities yesterday at Maggie's, but I grossly underestimated how much food I'd need. I should have bought three times what I purchased.

Jack's hovering over me in the kitchen, offering to help, but I keep trying to shoo him away. "Go sit down and eat. This kitchen isn't big enough for the both of us." But I say it with a smile, and as he passes me, he pats my ass, sending shivers up my spine.

Aleksa and Lenny are seated at the table, drinking coffee and scarfing down breakfast like they haven't eaten in a week. I offer them seconds, and then thirds, and they keep saying yes. At this rate, I'll run out of food soon.

Mike is on watch, seated by the front window with a rifle within reach. Diego is outside placing motion sensors along the driveway and in the woods.

"This siege had better not last long," I say, "or we'll run the risk of starving."

"Don't worry," Jack says. "Once it starts, it'll be over soon. We won't starve."

"I do have plenty of nonperishable rations in the pantry," I say. "We can survive a long time on beans and rice."

Jack returns to my side. "Sit down and eat. I'll take over here." He reaches across the cabinet for the coffee pot and refills my half-empty cup.

"Thanks," I say, picking up my mug.

He grabs a plate, fills it with food, and hands it to me. "You want some toast?" he asks as takes the spatula from me and turns the bacon in the skillet.

Jack seems to be going out of his way to be agreeable this morning. I guess that surprises me after our conversation last night, when I confessed to him that the only reason I slept with him was because I thought he was about to leave town.

I'm sitting at the table eating when I hear the rumble of an approaching engine. I recognize the familiar sound.

Mike grabs the rifle, as Lenny and Aleksa both draw their side arms. Even Jack is reaching for his holstered Glock.

"Wait!" I shoot to my feet. "It's just my brother, Micah."

They all ease their posture a bit, although they're clearly still on alert. Then it dawns on me that Diego is out there, in the woods, somewhere between the cabin and the road. He might mistake Micah for one of the mobsters. "Shit! Diego's out there." I'm out the door in a flash, running down the front steps.

"Ruth, wait!" Jack races outside after me, followed by Aleksa.

The sound of the motorcycle draws near, and I'm running across the yard and toward the gravel lane. "Don't shoot!" I yell, praying Diego can hear me. "Don't shoot!"

Just as Micah's bike rolls into view, Diego steps out of the trees, his handgun pointed right at my brother.

Micah's dressed in black and wearing a bike helmet with a tinted visor. Admittedly, he looks menacing.

"Don't shoot!" I yell, still running forward. "That's my brother!"

"Ruth, stop!" Jack yells as he races after me.

As Diego steps directly into his path, gun drawn, Micah rolls to a stop and raises both hands.

"It's okay, Diego," Jack calls. "Stand down."

Micah removes his helmet and glares at Jack. "What the fuck!"

Diego holsters his gun.

Everyone's standing here, out in the open. All seven of us.

"Who the hell are all these guys?" Micah asks me as he starts walking his bike toward the cabin.

I fall into step beside him. "They're friends of Jack's. They've come to help him with his *situation*."

Micah parks his bike next to my Jeep, then turns to face the rest of us, his hands on his hips. He makes an impressive sight, all six foot two of him, dressed in black. His hair is braided. His expression is tense, angry. "And exactly what *situation* is that?" he asks, directing his ire at Jack. "The fact that you have the Russian mob after you?"

Jack blows out a heavy breath. "These are former teammates of mine. They've come to give me backup." He points them out. "Mike, Aleksa, Lenny. And that's Diego."

"Are you expecting anyone else?" Diego asks me. "Is there a guest list I should know about? It would be nice to know ahead of time so we don't accidently kill your friends."

"I warned everyone to stay away," I say as I glare at my brother. "But apparently some people have problems following instructions."

Micah turns his dark eyes on me. "You really think I'd stay away when my own sister might be in danger?"

"We can handle this, Micah," Jack says. "You should—"

Micah jabs a finger in Jack's direction. "Don't tell me what to do. I'm not leaving my sister here unprotected."

"*I'll* protect her," Jack says.

"Who says I need protection?" I ask. "All of you—"

"Can we please take this discussion inside?" Mike asks, his voice remarkably calm in the face of so much testosterone. "We could have unwanted company any moment."

Grumbling, we all head back into the cabin. All except for Lenny, who grabs a sniper rifle and takes up a position in the barn loft window, which the guys have nicknamed *The Sniper's Nest*. "I'll take first watch," he says as he heads for the barn.

Once the rest of us are inside, Mike closes the door and turns the deadbolt.

"You shouldn't have come," I say to Micah. "I told you to stay away."

"Oh, sure." Micah directs his attention to me. "And since when do I listen to you?"

"Apparently, it runs in the family," Jack mutters, earning himself glares from both me and my brother.

Micah turns his attention to Jack. "Let me guess. The mob followed you to Bryce, and you're planning to have it out with them here at *my sister's house?* Have I got that right?"

"Pretty much," Jack says. "I've tried talking her into leaving town, but she refuses to go."

"Of course she does," Micah says. "Have you met my sister? She doesn't back down."

Jack sighs. "Micah, nothing's going to happen to Ruth."

Micah crosses his arms. "You bet nothing's going to

happen to her because I'm staying."

"No, you're not," I say, at the exact same time Jack says, "The hell you are!"

"I'm staying," Micah repeats. "End of discussion."

"Then you'll have to stay in the cabin," Mike says. He nods to the others. "We're a team. We're used to working together. You'd just get in our way."

"That's fine," Micah says. "I'm just here for Ruth. I brought fire power and ammo." He heads for the door. "It's outside in my satchel."

Micah brings in a backpack containing two handguns, a ton of ammo, and a vicious-looking knife. I follow him into my bedroom, where he unpacks everything and stows it on my dresser.

"I wish you hadn't come," I say. "This is a risky situation, and it's only going to get worse."

Micah pulls me into his arms. "That's exactly why I came. You may be my big sister, and when we were little you looked out for me. But now it's my turn." He gazes down at me. "I'm not letting you face this alone."

Micah and I return to the living room, where the guys are standing around the dining table, gazing down at a hand-drawn map of my property that someone scribbled onto the back of a brown paper bag. The main road, gravel lane, clearing, cabin and barn are clearly labeled with a black marker.

Diego points out strategic spots on the map. "I put motion sensors here, here, and here, as well as along the lane. If anyone comes up the lane—" He shoots a condescending look at Micah "—we'll know about it. If anyone comes out of the woods near the cabin, we'll know. I also put sensors along the exterior of the cabin and the barn."

Jack pats Diego's back. "Good job. Mike will take the sniper's nest, and I'll be positioned outside the cabin. The rest of you will patrol the woods around the cabin. Everyone stays on comms and checks in at regular intervals."

"When do you think they'll arrive?" I ask.

"As soon as it's dark," Jack says. "I imagine they're already here in town, just biding their time until nightfall."

"Then all hell breaks loose," Diego says, nodding in agreement as he consults his watch. "It won't be long now."

"How many do you think will come?" I ask.

"There's no way to know for sure, but I'd guess around ten, maybe a dozen."

"But there's only *five* of you. Seven if you include me and Micah."

He smiles. "Trust me. No matter how many they

bring, it won't be a fair fight."

When I frown, he says, "No, you misunderstand me. This will be a cakewalk for my guys. My main concern is for the safety of you and your brother."

* * *

When early evening comes, I make dinner for everyone—burgers. Something quick as we don't have much time left before sunset. These guys sure can pack away a lot of food.

It amazes me how, even faced with such odds, they still have the capacity to joke with each other. Even with me.

They take turns watching at the front window. Currently, Lenny's on duty.

16

Jack

After dinner, we finish our preparations.

Ruth has her guns and ammo laid out on the counter in the bathroom. Micah has set up his small arsenal in Ruth's bedroom, where he can keep an eye on the east side of the cabin, as well as on his sister.

At the moment, the bathroom door is open, and I stand there taking in Ruth's arrangement of her shotgun and two 9mm handguns. She's in the process of arranging boxes of ammo and loading spare magazines for the 9mm's.

"You doing okay?" I ask.

She glances at me, her expression remarkably calm. This woman is hard to rattle. "Yes. I just never thought I'd have an occasion to use these things."

"Ruth—" There's so much I want to say, but now isn't the time. The shit's about to hit the fan any minute now. We can't afford any distractions.

"Yes?" she asks.

I step into the small room to inspect her preparations. Besides the guns and ammo, she has a couple of bottles of spring water and some protein bars. I have to smile. "You look prepared for anything." I reach for her hand, and surprisingly, she lets me have it.

She surveys the black vest strapped to my torso, as well as the one I'm holding in my free hand. "Is that what I think it is?"

"It's body armor." I lift up the spare. "I want you to wear this. It's bulletproof."

She eyes the vest, then me. "Okay."

"What!" I pretend to be shocked. "You're not going to argue with me about it?"

She makes a wry face. "I may be stubborn, but I don't have a death wish."

Ruth stands perfectly still as I strap the vest to her torso, cinching it tight.

After examining the fit, I stand back to observe. "This will protect most of your vital organs."

She frowns. "But not my head, obviously."

"True. But the point is, you're going to stay indoors where you'll be safe. I won't let Yevgeny or his men breach the cabin. And since you've got Micah in here with you for backup, you'll be fine." I reach into my front pocket and pull out a surveillance comm device.

"One last thing," I say as I clip the comm device to her vest and tuck the power pack in her pocket. "This is a two-way radio. You'll be able to hear everything we say with this, and in the event of an emergency, you can speak to us by pushing this button here. Otherwise, just listen in."

On impulse, I take her hand in mine. "When the shooting starts, you keep out of sight, no matter what you hear. I can't do what I need to do out there if I'm worried about you, all right?"

She nods. "I will."

I squeeze her hand hard to make my point. "I need

you to promise me, Ruth."

"I'm not stupid, Jack. This is all way over my pay grade."

"Good. Keep that promise." And then, because I can't help myself, I throw caution to the wind and move in to kiss her.

To my surprise, she kisses me back, unreservedly, her soft lips clinging to mine. No snarky remarks, no recriminations. She *kisses* me.

"Now you promise *me* something," she says, pulling back and looking me directly in the eye. "Promise me you'll come back in one piece."

I nod. "I'll do my best."

She doesn't look happy with my reply, but instead of giving me crap over it, she leans in and gives me a peck on the cheek. "You'd damn well better."

I press the talk button on my comms device. "Comms check," I say over the radio. "Bravo 1."

"Bravo 2," Mike says.

"Bravo 3," Aleksa says.

"Bravo 4," Diego says.

"Saved the best for last," Lenny says with a soft chuckle. "Bravo 5."

"Ruth, try your mic." I say.

"Hello? Can you guys hear me?" she replies.

"Loud and clear," I say. "You're fine. Micah?"

"Yeah, I'm here," he replies.

"Good. Let's keep the line open and quiet. Once the op is underway, Bravo Team, I want you to check in every fifteen minutes."

And then the comms go quiet as we wait.

17

Ruth

As we're sitting around the table, biding our time, Diego's phone starts buzzing. He stands and stares at his phone screen. "Someone just pulled off the main road onto the lane. It's game time."

And just like that, Mike kills the lights in the cabin, thrusting us into darkness.

"Mike—" Jack says.

"Heading there now," Mike says, grabbing his rifle. He's on sniper duty in the barn loft.

"Ruth, go," Jack says, pushing me toward the bathroom.

Micah meets me halfway, steers me to my makeshift safe room, and follows me inside. "Stay in here," he says. He puts his hands on my shoulders and turns me to face him. "I'll be right outside your door. I won't let anyone get near you, I promise."

"Who's going to protect *you*?" I ask.

He grins at me. "How many times did you have my back when we were kids? You were always looking out for me. Now it's my turn to return the favor."

I have to tilt my head up to meet Micah's gaze. "Please be careful," I say. "If something happened to you—"

"Nothing's going to happen to me, sis." He pulls me close for a hug, his arms wrapping securely around me. It's an awkward embrace as we're both wearing body armor. He steps back through the open doorway. "Lock this door." And then he closes it.

Even as I lock the door, I realize this flimsy barrier would be little protection against someone determined to get through. My heart is thundering as I begin pacing the small space. There's hardly room for me to take five steps before I have to pivot and return to where I started. I try not to look at my reflection in the mirror over the vanity. The sight of the bulletproof vest is a frightening reminder of what's about to happen. And Jack and the others are *outside*, with little protection.

My stomach twists into knots as I contemplate our current situation. Any one of these guys could get hurt, or worse. The thought of something happening to Jack makes me ill.

I continue pacing, far too antsy to sit on the edge of the bathtub. Five minutes pass, then ten, then twenty, and I haven't heard a sound, not within the cabin or outside. The waiting, the not knowing, is nerve-wracking.

The need to know what's going on gets the best of me. I press my ear to the bathroom door and listen. When I don't hear anything, I quietly unlock the door and ease it open, just enough that I can peer outside.

I spot a shadow standing to the side of the front window, just out of sight. It's Micah.

It's fully dark out now, the only illumination coming from a full moon.

Suddenly, I hear a soft crackle over my earpiece.

"Three black SUVs coming up the lane," Diego says in a steady, even voice.

"I see them," Aleksa says.

"I'm in position," Jack says. "In the woods across from the cabin porch."

"I'm watching the cabin," Lenny says.

"In the nest," Mike confirms.

Before long, Micah and I can hear the distinct crunch of tires on gravel as the vehicles slowly progress up the lane.

"I need a headcount," Jack says.

"They've stopped about halfway up the lane," Diego reports. "They're getting out. Looks like they're going the rest of the way on foot."

"I count nine," Aleksa says. "No, wait. Ten. All heavily armed."

"Do you see Yevgeny?" Jack asks.

"Hard to tell," Aleksa says. "They're all wearing masks."

Suddenly the comms go quiet, and my heart starts pounding even harder. Any second now, there might be gunfire. Any second now, someone might get hurt. Or worse.

Micah puts his arm around me and holds me to him. "It'll be okay," he whispers.

But he can't know that for sure. He's just trying to placate me.

"Get back in the bathroom," he says quietly, nudging me in that direction.

But I'm rooted to the spot, unable to turn away. To

hide.

Pop pop pop

Gunfire.

Then quiet for the space of several heartbeats.

Suddenly, there's a barrage of shots, coming from the left of us, down the lane. Men dressed in dark clothing emerge from the lane into the clearing, darting away to take cover behind trees, beside my Jeep, beside the SUV parked across the yard.

The mobsters are firing into the trees, and the trees are firing back.

When one of the assailants attempts to breach the front porch, a shot rings out, and the mobster falls backward onto the ground, where he lies still.

Another barrage of gunfire is followed by a spate of silence. Two of the goons race for the porch steps, one of them stopped dead in his tracks by a shot to the back of his head. The other races back to hide in front of my Jeep.

There are two dead bodies lying just beyond my porch.

Micah grips my left arm. "Go, Ruth. To the safe room."

All I can do is shake my head and watch, horrified, out the window. "What if someone's been shot?" I ask, my voice no more than a whisper.

"Bravo Two?" It's Jack's voice. He's breathing heavily.

"Here," someone says. I think that's Mike.

"Bravo Three?" Jack again.

"Here." That's definitely Aleksa.

"Bravo Four?"

"Here." Diego.

"Bravo Five?"

"Here," says a raspy voice. Lenny. But something's wrong. He's breathing hard. No, he's gasping. "Fuck, I'm hit." He groans.

"Hold on, Lenny," Jack says. "I'll come get you."

Suddenly, Lenny comes from around the corner of the cabin, his hand pressed hard to his side. I see blood seeping between his fingers. As he staggers up the porch steps, shots ring out, ricocheting off the wood railing. Lenny ducks, trying to keep a low profile as he makes a dash for the cabin door.

I race for the door.

"Ruth, no!" Micah yells. "Don't open that door!"

"I have to! He's hurt, Micah." I turn the deadbolt and release the chain so I can open the door.

Grimacing in pain, Lenny lurches inside.

I lunge forward, hoping to catch him before he falls, but he quickly rights himself and draws a semi-automatic handgun, which he points at my head.

I'm confused. "Lenny?"

"Stay back, Micah," Lenny says in a hard voice. He keeps his gun trained on me. "Or she's dead. Whether I shoot her now or later doesn't make any difference to me."

Micah lays his own gun on the windowsill, raises his hands, and takes several steps back. "Fine. Just don't hurt her."

I look from Lenny to Micah and back. Lenny looks perfectly calm and determined. I glance at his side and realize there's no wound there, only blood smeared on his clothing. "Lenny, what are you doing?"

Lenny grabs my arm, pulls me to him, and shoves the muzzle of his gun against my temple. "If you move an inch, Micah, I promise you I'll shoot her."

Micah's face hardens into a mask of cold rage as he clenches his hands at his sides. His gaze remains locked on Lenny. "You're not going to get away with this."

Lenny kicks the front door wide open and shoves me through it, out onto the porch. He stands directly behind me, holding me in front of him like I'm some kind of human shield. "Come on out, Jack!" he yells. "Unless you want your girlfriend's death on your hands, you'd better show yourself."

18

Ruth

The woods around my cabin are suddenly quiet. The fighting has stopped. The only sound I hear is my own breathing, which is loud and raspy to my own ears.

Lenny shoves me forward, tipping me off balance, and I nearly fall face first, but he catches me and hauls me back up to my feet. He wraps one arm securely around my waist, holding me against him, and points his gun at my temple.

Well, I think we know who the mole is now.

Jack emerges from the woods across the clearing, his empty hands in the air. His dark gaze is locked on me. "Don't hurt her, Lenny." His voice is surprisingly quiet, the words deadly. "Don't give me a reason to end you."

"Get over here," Lenny shouts. "Put your hands on your head and turn around, slowly."

Jack does exactly as Lenny instructs.

"Lenny, please don't do this," I say, my voice breaking.

"Get up here!" Lenny yells.

Jack walks toward the porch, his steps slow and deliberate.

Tears prickle my eyes when I realize what's happening. Lenny's going to make Jack surrender to these mobsters. My gaze locks onto Jack, whose face is expressionless. I shake my head. "Jack, don't! Please, don't." He can't just give himself up, not on my account. He can't just lie down and let them murder him in cold blood.

Jack gazes back at me, but says nothing. When he reaches the porch steps, he takes them one at a time, slowly ascending until he's right in front of me. He looks me in the eye, utterly calm, which makes my blood run cold.

He's going to do this! He's going to let them take him.

"It's going to be okay, Ruth," Jack says quietly.

"That's a bit premature, don't you think?" Lenny asks, his voice snide and hateful.

"Get the gun off her, Len," Jack says in a steady voice. "Point it at me."

"Don't tell me what to do!" Lenny snaps. "You think you're so fucking high and mighty. The perfect Jack Merchant, the *Merchant of Death*. Well, now who's in charge?"

"You are, Lenny," Jack says. "You've got the gun. You're in charge. Now, let Ruth go. You don't need her anymore. You have me."

A shrill whistle rends the air, causing Lenny to flinch, and in a flash of movement too fast for me to follow, Jack grabs Lenny's gun hand, twists it hard enough to snap bone, and wrenches the gun free. Jack fires the gun into Lenny's skull, dropping him on the spot.

"Not so fast, Merchant!" a deep voice growls. This one heavily accented. "Drop your weapon."

I glance past Jack to see several strangers pointing their guns right at us.

Jack looks me in the eye. "I need you to trust me," he says. "I won't let them hurt you." Then he tosses the gun he took from Lenny into the grass below us.

"Now turn around and face me," the big man says.

"Slowly. If you reach for a weapon, you and the woman die."

Jack turns to face Yuri, positioning himself squarely in front of me. "Stay behind me," he says tersely.

"You've been very difficult to pin down, Jack Merchant," the man says. He's tall, at least six feet, and built like a Mack truck. He's wearing a black overcoat, a black suit underneath.

"You must be Yuri," Jack says.

The big man nods. "*Da.*"

"You know," Jack says, "the irony of this is that I was never coming after you. It was Antonin who had to go. Not you."

"*Not yet*, you mean," Yuri says. "It was only a matter of time before your rifle was pointed at *my* head." Yuri laughs. "Now there are half a dozen guns pointed at your head."

Yuri points his gun right at Jack's head. "Where are the others? Call them out."

Jack just stands there, saying nothing.

"There were five of you in all, but now poor Lenny is dead, so there's only four left. You plus three others." Yuri glances around the clearing. "Come out, death squad, all of you, or I'll put a bullet in your friend's brain."

My heart sinks when I see Diego step out of the woods, his empty hands on top of his head. *Oh, God, no. They can't just give up.*

"Come on!" Yuri yells. "I'm not a patient man. Two more!"

Aleksa shows himself, stepping out from behind the barn. His hands are on his head, too.

"Better," Yuri says. "One more."

Mike is the only one who hasn't shown himself. Mike, who's up in the sniper's nest. He has a clear shot at everyone in the clearing. A clear shot at Yuri.

"I'm losing my patience!" Yuri growls. "I want the last one out here, now, or I start shooting. As soon as Merchant falls, then the woman is next."

Mike, shoot him. Do it!

When I hear a movement coming from behind me in the cabin, I glance back to see Micah standing in the open doorway, his empty hands at his sides. "Micah, no!"

Jack tightens his grip on me.

"I'm here," Micah says loudly, his voice carrying as he steps out onto the porch.

My heart is ripping to shreds as the sound of rushing blood fills my ears.

It wasn't supposed to happen this way.

Jack turns to me, his hands cupping my face. "It's okay, Ruth," he says.

My voice breaks. "How can you say that?"

Jack flashes Micah a quick look before he turns to face Yuri.

"Get down here," Yuri tells Jack. "On your knees in front of me."

As Jack takes a step forward, a single shot rings out, shattering the stillness. Almost in slow motion, blood spurts from the side of Yuri's head and he drops to his knees before he falls back, his head hitting the ground. His cold, lifeless eyes stare up at the night sky.

Jack throws me down onto the porch boards and covers me with his body. Micah draws a 9mm from his back waistband and starts firing. Gunfire erupts all throughout the yard, accompanied by shouts and cries of pain. The deafening noise goes on and on, as if time has slowed, until eventually it dies down.

"Take her," Jack says to Micah as he raises himself off me.

Micah grabs me under my arms and hauls me into the cabin. He shuts the door behind us and locks it.

"You idiot!" I reach for my brother and hug him tightly, shaken by the incredible risk he took. "You could have been killed."

"Any of us could have been killed tonight," Micah says. "But my money was on Mike. As long as he was up there in the barn loft, we had an ace up our sleeve."

When we're both assured the other is unharmed, we move to the window and peer out into the moonlit yard. Jack, Diego, and Aleksa are dragging fallen bodies to the center of the clearing, lining them up on the ground. I glance up at the sniper's nest and see the muzzle of Mike's rifle trained on the yard.

"Ten!" Aleksa calls. "We got them all."

I guess that's the all-clear sign because, a moment later, Mike Roman strolls out of the barn, holding his rifle at the ready, just in case.

There's a knock on the front door. I open it.

Jack walks in, a big grin on his face. "Now you can call the sheriff," he tells me. And then he pulls me into his arms and squeezes the daylights out of me. "Are you okay?"

"I'm fine," I say. "What about you?"

"Not a scratch on me."

"Were you serious about me calling the sheriff?"

He nods. "Sure. Somebody's got to deal with all these bodies. Besides, we're in the clear. It was self-defense."

Jack goes back outside to check on his teammates. Aleksa and Diego both have minor injuries. Jack and Mike are fine.

Micah remains inside with me.

"What you did tonight was incredibly brave, but very risky," I finally say to him. I walk to the fridge and grab us each a bottle of beer. I pop the caps and hand him one.

"I had to do it," Micah says. "We needed Mike up there in the sniper's nest. I knew if he took out Yuri, it would be over quickly."

I take a long swig of my beer and realize my hand is shaking.

Micah notices, too. "It's a delayed reaction to the stress."

I laugh. "Ya think?"

He reaches out and brushes my cheek. "Jack really stepped up. He was ready to sacrifice himself for you."

I nod. "Yes, he did." He used his own *body* to protect me.

Micah pulls out his phone. "I'll call Chris." While he's talking to the overnight dispatcher, Jack and the guys walk inside.

"Can I get you boys something to drink?" I ask, slipping into my familiar role, but instead of a bar between us, it's my kitchen counter.

Jack eyes my beer bottle. "Have you got anything stronger?"

"Yes," I say, laughing. I open the door to a cupboard to the right of my fridge. Inside are half a dozen bottles of top shelf liquor.

Jack catches my gaze. "I'll have my usual," he says with a grin.

"Coming right up." I grab a tumbler, pour him a double shot of whiskey, and hand it to him.

"Same for me," Mike says.

I end up pouring a double shot of whiskey for all four of the death squad members.

Twenty minutes later, the sheriff's SUV pulls into my yard, along with two police cruisers.

The six of us head outside to greet Sheriff Chris Nelson and explain the circumstances.

Jack shakes Chris's hand, and then he proceeds to tell him everything.

Suddenly, I'm exhausted. I stoke the fire and take a seat on the sofa. My head is spinning, thoughts racing as the events of the night flash over and over through my head. Each time, I realize how close we came to disaster.

Each time, I remember Jack putting himself between

me and Yuri. I remember him taking me down to the porch and covering me with his body. The man risked his own life for mine.

I lean my head back on the cushions and close my eyes, hoping the room will stop spinning. The heat radiating from the wood stove feels good, comforting me.

Someone reaches for my hand. "Hey."

I open my eyes to find Jack sitting on the coffee table, facing me, cradling my hand in both of his.

He brushes the back of my hand. "You okay?"

I shrug, too tired to pretend otherwise. "Everything keeps playing in a loop."

He sighs. "That's typical. It was a rough night, and you've been through a lot."

I think of the ten dead bodies lying in my front yard. "You could say that." I lean forward and take both of his hands in mine. "You risked your life for me tonight."

Now it's his turn to shrug. "It was nothing."

"That wasn't *nothing*, Jack." I sit forward, facing him, our knees just inches apart.

His expression falls. "Don't forget, I'm the one who got you into this mess in the first place."

He's so determined to downplay his heroism tonight. "And you got me out of it, too." When I reach out and cup his cheek, he closes his eyes, as if savoring my touch. I lean closer and kiss him, pressing my lips lightly to his.

Before he can respond, Mike walks into the cabin. "Sorry, Jack, but the sheriff wants to see you."

I sit back on the sofa as Jack nods to his friend.

"I'll be right there," he says. He rises to his feet. "It's late," he says to me. "You should try to get some sleep. We'll wrap up outside."

Once he's gone, I walk to the window and peer outside. Chris has a spotlight shining down on the bodies, which have been covered with black tarps. There's a coroner's wagon in the yard now.

Micah comes inside. "That's a logistical nightmare. Ten bodies. That's a lot for a small county to deal with. They're calling in to other counties for assistance. It'll be a few hours before all the bodies are taken away." He walks up beside me. "Go to bed, Ruth. I'll stay up and keep a tab on things. You need sleep."

I'm exhausted, and I don't know how much longer I can stay upright. "I think I will. Let me know if you need me for anything."

"Will do," Micah says. He gives me a hug and kisses the top of my head.

After a pit stop in the bathroom to get ready for bed,

I go to my room, shut the door, and collapse onto the mattress. I don't even bother to undress. I'm too tired, too shaken.

Sleep is slow in coming, and when it does, it comes in fits and starts. My head is filled with nightmare images of Micah being shot, Jack, or the others. It's a miracle none of them was seriously hurt tonight.

* * *

I wake early, before the sun is fully up, stunned when I realize I slept through the night. I'm a bit surprised to find I'm alone in my bed. I wouldn't have been surprised if I'd awakened to find Jack in bed with me.

After using the bathroom, I walk out into the main living area. Micah's asleep on the sofa, his long legs sticking out on one side. I try not to wake him as I start making coffee. There's no sign of Jack, so I imagine he's still asleep in the guest bedroom.

I glance out the kitchen window to see Mike heading across the yard, toward the cabin. I unlock the door and open it for him so he doesn't have to knock.

"Good morning," I whisper as he walks in.

He nods. "Morning," he replies just as quietly. He

glances toward the kitchen. "Coffee?"

"I just put it on. It won't take long."

Mike glances at the sofa, spotting my brother's head resting on the arm. Then he looks me over. "You okay this morning?"

"Yes. I actually slept through the night. I guess exhaustion will do that to you."

By the time the coffee's ready, Diego and Aleksa have already joined us. Micah's awake now, sitting bleary-eyed on the sofa.

"How about some breakfast?" I ask the group. I see a lot of grateful nods. "Someone should wake Jack," I say, "or he'll miss out on all the fun."

Mike looks me in the eye. "Ruth."

My stomach drops at the tone of his voice. "Yes?"

"Jack's gone. He left early this morning, right after the sheriff and the coroners finished up."

"*Left?*" My gut hollows out. *He left without saying goodbye? Without even telling me?* "Where'd he go?"

Instead of answering my question, Mike pulls a folded piece of paper from his back pocket and hands it to me. "He left you this."

I make it as far as the kitchen table before I collapse onto one of the chairs.

He's gone.

I guess I shouldn't be surprised. He said the reason he stayed was because he was worried about my safety. Since that's no longer an issue, there's no reason for him to hang around.

I unfold the note.

Ruth,

I'm sorry for everything I put you through. I hope you believe that. And if you don't, well, I can't really blame you.

I've gone to make things right.

Thanks for everything,
Jack

I blink back the tears making it difficult for me to read, refold the note, and stick it in my back pocket. "Well, I guess that's that." *What else can I say?*

I'm such a hypocrite. I made it clear I didn't want him to stay—that I didn't want a relationship—and yet his leaving like this feels like a knife in my heart.

Mike's leaning against the kitchen counter, his arms crossed over his chest, watching me, as if he's expecting me to fall apart. *That's not going to happen.*

"I'm sure he had his reasons," Mike says, apologizing on Jack's behalf.

I level my gaze on him. "He left without saying a word, after everything we—" I stop because I'm getting choked up, and I am not going to fall apart in front of these guys.

Mike gestures to the note. "Not exactly."

"How about if I make breakfast?" Aleksa asks as he walks up behind me. He gently squeezes my shoulders. "You've already done so much for us, Ruth. You should take it easy and rest."

"After breakfast, we'll pack up our gear and load the vehicles," Mike says. "We'll be out of your hair in no time."

19

Jack

At four that morning, I drove to the Denver International Airport, parked the Impala, and caught the first flight to La Guardia. Yuri Yevgeny was no longer in the picture, but that didn't mean my troubles were over. As soon as word got back to the organization that Yuri was dead, someone would have moved in immediately to fill the vacuum. I just don't know who. To the best of my knowledge, there are no more Yevgeny brothers waiting in the wings. Maybe a cousin, perhaps. Maybe someone back in Russia. But I'm not aware of anyone.

The Yevgeny operation is headquartered in a five-star hotel in the Bronx—the seat of Yevgeny's power. I walk into the hotel—garnering a lot of strange looks from the staff. Immediately, I'm confronted by security. One of the guys frisks me while another watches dispassionately. They're probably hoping I'm carrying so they have an excuse to shoot me. When they realize I'm empty-handed, they let me continue on into the bar, although I can feel their eyes on me every second.

I take a seat at the bar, front and center, and wait. Two armed security guards take up positions behind me.

It's not long before a man dressed in an Armani suit claims the empty barstool next to mine. "Hello, Mr. Merchant," he says as he lights a cigar. "Welcome back to The Big Apple."

I glance at the man next to me. He's probably in his mid-forties, blond hair, blue eyes, tall and fit. "And you are?" I ask.

He offers me his hand, and we shake. "Vladmir Pavlenko. You may call me Vlad."

"First name basis, already? I suppose you're the one in charge around here now."

DARK AND DANGEROUS 181

"Yes," he says, very matter-of-fact. He takes a puff on his cigar, then blows a cloud of smoke into the air. "I took advantage of a recent opening in management."

"I see."

A bartender approaches and takes our orders. Vodka for Vlad. Not a surprise there. "I'll have a whiskey, double, neat."

"Yes, sir," the bartender says, and then he proceeds to prepare our drinks. He hands Pavlenko his first, then mine to me.

"So, what brings you to my hotel?" Pavlenko asks.

"I wanted to find out if you have a problem with me."

Pavlenko puffs on his cigar. "I guess that depends."

"On?"

"On whether or not *you* have a problem with *me*."

I take a sip of my whiskey, relishing the burn as it slides down my throat. "I do not."

"Well, then," he says, "it seems we are in agreement."

"Glad to hear it." I knock back the rest of my drink, then pull out my wallet.

"That won't be necessary," Pavlenko says. "It's on the house. Consider it a token of my gratitude."

Gratitude? Inwardly, I chuckle. *Yes, I guess he does have me to thank for the promotion.* I stand and slip my wallet into my back pocket. "Have a nice life, Mr. Pavlenko. If you don't mind me saying so, I hope we never cross paths again."

"I agree wholeheartedly, Mr. Merchant."

* * *

After leaving the hotel, I walk for a while, taking in the sights and sounds of the Bronx. It's lunch time, so I stop in for authentic New York pizza.

I keep an eye out for any potential tails, but there isn't one. It appears Pavlenko meant what he said. We have no problem with each other.

It's over.

I can go live my life without a guillotine hanging over my neck.

It hits me that I'm free to go anywhere, do anything. Most importantly, I'm free to settle down somewhere and establish roots. I can finally take steps working toward what I've wanted for a long time.

Having given it a lot of thought this past week, I've decided to try my hand at bartending. I think I'd be good at that. With a plan in place, I grab a taxi and head back to the airport.

20

Ruth

The day Mike and the guys left town, they assured me the danger had passed. There was nothing for me—or my town—to worry about. They hung around the cabin until early afternoon that day, for no apparent reason. And then, after Mike received a brief phone call, he declared it was time for them to hit the road.

I had to wonder if it was Jack who made that call.

There are tears in my eyes when we all hug and say

our goodbyes. Although I haven't known these guys for long, they did put their lives on the line partly for me. And, they're my last link to Jack. As I watch them drive away in their SUVs, I feel oddly bereft.

It's over.

I should feel relieved. Glad even. But all I can think is, *he's gone. They're all gone.*

After deciding to keep the bar closed for one more day, I spend the next few hours trying to keep busy around the cabin, doing mundane chores like laundry and chopping more wood. I even take a walk in the woods in an attempt to clear my head. It doesn't really help.

Early that evening, Hannah McIntyre calls to invite me to have dinner with her and her partner, Killian Devereaux, at The Lodge. I jump at the chance to see some of my friends. It's a much-needed distraction.

When I arrive at The Lodge, I head straight to the restaurant. The hostess greets me and shows me to Hannah's table.

Hannah jumps to her feet when she spots me. "Are you okay?" she asks as we hug. She releases me and steps back so she can look me over. "And what about Micah? I heard he was there, too."

"I'm fine," I say as we take our seats. "We both are."

There's already an open bottle of red wine on the table. Hannah pours us each a glass. "Is it true Jack's gone? They're all gone?"

I nod as I take a sip. "Jack left in the wee hours this morning, and the rest of them left earlier this afternoon."

She peppers me with questions about the big showdown. About Jack and his friends. I fill her in as best I can, leaving out the gruesome details of the ten dead bodies lying in my front yard.

I tell her about the note Jack left me.

"Seriously?" Hannah asks. "He just up and left without even speaking to you?"

"Yep." I sound matter-of-fact, but my heart is aching. "I should be grateful. I told him I wasn't looking for a relationship. It was supposed to be a one-night thing, but then the shit hit the fan the next morning, and he couldn't leave as he'd planned. He saved me the trouble of asking him to leave."

Hannah reaches for my hand and squeezes it. "I'm so sorry, Ruth."

Killian joins us then. "Sorry," he says, a bit breathless as he sits. "I was on the phone with Chris. He gave me a run down on what happened last night at your cabin, Ruth. The coroner's office is slammed with making arrangements to return the bodies to New York." He shakes his head. "I can't believe this happened in our own backyard." And then he gives me a look. "You didn't even call us for help."

"Jack told me not to involve anyone else, not even Chris," I say. "He said it was too dangerous. And based on what I witnessed, I'd say he was right. There was a lot of crossfire. It was chaotic, and one of you could have gotten hurt. I could never live with that."

Our server comes to take our orders and fill our coffee cups.

"It's a miracle you weren't hurt," Hannah says.

"I can thank Jack for that," I admit. "He planted himself between me and Yuri, the mob boss. He could have easily died."

I change the subject at that point because talking about Jack, even thinking about him, hurts too much.

"When are you going to reopen the bar?" Hannah asks.

"I guess tomorrow," I say. "There's no reason not to. And I could do with some normalcy right now."

* * *

It's amazing how quickly everything gets back to normal. I show up at the bar the next day around two o'clock in the afternoon to make sure everything's ready. Tom shows up shortly after, followed by the kitchen staff, and lastly the servers and Casey.

I'm in my office getting a cash deposit ready to take to the bank when our lead cook, Jerome, knocks on my open office door. "We've got a problem, Ruth."

"What kind of problem?" After what I've been through the past twenty-four hours, I doubt Jerome's problem is that serious in comparison.

"Steve just texted me to tell me he's quitting. No notice, no warning. We'll need to hire another dishwasher ASAP. Do you want me to post a job opening?"

In the scheme of things, being short a dishwasher for a day or two isn't the end of the world. Tom and I can take turns filling in. Or maybe Casey, if he has time. "Yes, please post a job opening. The sooner the better."

A few moments later, Tom walks into my office. "I just heard about Steve quitting. What are we going to do about the dishes until we hire someone new?"

And just that like, it's back to business as usual, as if nothing ever happened. As if ten mobsters weren't killed on my property. As if my brother didn't risk his life to help us. As if Jack didn't position himself directly between me and a mob boss, willing to take a bullet to protect me. I shudder at the image of Yuri shooting Jack.

"You and I will have to take turns," I say.

Tom shakes his head. "I'll handle the dishes until we get someone in here. You worry about the bar."

"All right. But I hate for you to—"

"Hey, it's honest work," he says. "And it needs to be done, or the kitchen will come crashing to a halt, and we'll have some hangry customers on our hands."

I smile for the first time in nearly two days. "You're a good man, Tom."

At the top of the hour, I'm standing behind the bar when Tom turns on the OPEN sign and unlocks the front door. There's already a line outside our door, visible halfway down the block. I think folks are mostly curious and looking for gossip after the local paper ran a story about organized crime showing up in our small town. Business is booming all afternoon, and orders are keeping me on my toes.

Tom bounces back and forth from the kitchen to the bar, trying to be in two places at once. "I wish people wouldn't eat so much," he grouses. "The dirty dishes just keep coming."

I chuckle. "Hey, those food orders pay our bills. Don't knock it."

All afternoon, I keep catching Tom watching me with a worried look on his face.

"I'm fine, Tom," I tell him. "It's over. It's done. *I'm fine.*"

I'm not sure he believes me.

Around seven, after the initial dinner rush is over, I sneak out and head next door to the diner. When she spots me coming in, Jenny motions me to a table for two along the outside wall.

She drops into the empty chair with a sigh. "How are you doing?" Before I can reply, she holds up a finger. "Wait. Hold that thought. Can I get you something to eat or drink?"

"Thanks, but I'm not hungry. I just needed a break. The bar has been swamped today. And Chrissy and Jess keep asking me about Jack—why he left so abruptly and where he went—and I just don't have any answers for them."

"So, he's really gone? Just like that?"

"Yep."

"He didn't even say goodbye?"

"He left me a note."

"What'd he say?"

"Basically, 'have a nice life. Sorry for the inconvenience.'"

Jenny frowns. "Ouch. Seriously, that's it?"

I shrug. "He said something about making things right."

"What does that mean?"

"I have no idea."

The door that connects the diner to the grocery store opens, and Maggie walks through. "I saw you come in," she says when she reaches our table. She leans down to give me a hug. "I can't stay. I wanted to say hi and tell you I'm so sorry. I heard about what happened at your cabin the other night. You're all right, though? Micah, too?"

I nod. "We're fine."

"Did you hear that Jack up and left in the middle of the night, without a word to Ruth?" Jenny asks.

Maggie winces. "I did hear something along those lines."

I shake my head. "Word sure travels fast in this town."

Maggie gives me another hug and squeezes my shoulder. "Call if you need anything. I've got to run. Owen's working with me in the store this evening, but we've got Claire with us, and she's teething again, so she's not a happy camper."

Maggie walks back through the connecting door to

her shop.

"Are you sure you don't want anything to eat?" Jenny says. "How about pot roast with warm rolls and fresh butter? Pure comfort food. Or we've got chicken pot pie served with mashed potatoes and gravy? Or how about some warm apple pie with vanilla ice cream on top?"

I smile at my friend. Food is love, and Jenny has lots of love to give. "The pot roast sounds great, thank you."

"And apple pie?"

I nod. "Yes, and apple pie."

It's eight-thirty by the time I return to the bar. Things have quieted down now, the crowd has thinned out. Most of the sightseers and gawkers have left. Tom's got the bar under control, and the servers are busy racing back and forth with customer orders. Casey is bussing tables, and Taylor Swift is belting out an oldie-but-goodie on the jukebox.

It definitely looks like everything's back to normal. I should be glad, relieved even, but instead I can't shake this feeling of emptiness. I feel like something's missing. Lost.

My gaze goes automatically to the end of the bar to see Jack's seat conspicuously empty.

He really is gone, and I have no one to blame but myself. I never really gave him a chance. I never gave him any reason to stay.

Chrissy taps my shoulder and nods to the front end of the bar. "I think there's someone here to see you."

I turn to look, and my heart slams into my ribs at the sight of Jack, with an amused grin on his face. He looks amazing. And happy.

He offers me his hand, and we shake, his grip firm. Just one touch from him sends shivers through me.

"Jack Merchant," he says. "Pleased to meet you."

"What are you doing here?" I ask.

He shrugs. "Let's start with looking for work. I was wondering if you could use another bartender."

I can't take my eyes off him. My pulse is thundering, and my head is spinning. "Where were you?"

"I went to New York City. To the Bronx, actually."

"Why?"

"To find out if I still had a price on my head."

"And do you?"

He shakes his head. "Apparently not. The new boss and I have zero interest in each other. In fact, he bought me a drink as a thank-you."

"A thank-you for what?"

"For creating a power vacuum in The Big Apple that

he could take advantage of. He absorbed the Yevgeny organization into his own, practically doubling its size and power. But we're good. We have an agreement. I'll leave them alone, and they'll leave me alone."

I realize that's good news, of course, and I admit to being thrilled to see him again, but underneath all the excitement is hurt. "You left without saying anything. Not even goodbye." I didn't mean to bring that up because it sounds so *needy*, but the words just came out, and yes, they are tinged with resentment.

"I'm sorry. I guess a note didn't cut it." His smile falls. "I had to be sure I was in the clear before I could see you again and try to make amends. I couldn't put you through something like what happened here. Not again. So, about the bartender job. Were you serious when you mentioned it before?"

My impulse is to say *yes*! I want him here. I want him to stay. But that's such a risky leap for me. I can't go from all-out to all-in practically overnight. I still have my misgivings about trying again. "I was joking about the bartending job," I say. I feel like shit when his smile fades. "But we do have an opening for a dishwasher. If you—"

"Fine, I'll take it," he says, sighing so dramatically I have to bite my lip not to smile. "I'll wash dishes. I'll take out the trash. I'll do whatever you want." His dark eyes lock onto mine. "I want us to start over, Ruth."

My throat tightens painfully at the sincerity I hear in his voice. I want so badly to say *yes*. To take the do-over. To *try*.

"The shift is from four to midnight," I say. "Minimum wage, paid every Friday. You can start tonight, now in fact, if you want to. Report to Jerome in the kitchen. He'll give you a quick orientation."

"All right." He sounds disappointed, yet resigned. "Dishwasher, it is." With a salute, he heads for the kitchen.

I remain frozen on the spot. Stunned.

Chrissy, who'd been loitering at the bar so she could listen in, is smiling. "Oh, he's got it bad for you." She shakes her head as she picks up a tray of beer bottles and walks away.

21

Jack

"You're pullin' my leg, aren't you, son?" Tom asks after I walk into the kitchen and tell him I'm the new dishwasher.

"Nope." I shrug off my leather jacket, hang it on a coat rack behind the door, and start rolling up my sleeves. "Ruth just hired me. I start now."

Tom looks skeptical. "I don't suppose you have any experience operating a commercial dishwashing station."

I laugh. "I've washed more than a few dishes in my

lifetime, Tom. How hard can it be?"

He gestures to the industrial set-up in front of him. "This isn't the same as washing dishes in your kitchen sink."

I scan the washing station, which does look rather elaborate. In addition to a huge stainless steel box sitting on the counter, there are racks and tubs filled with dirty dishes, mugs, glasses, and silverware. "I'm a fast learner," I say. "Just break it all down for me."

Tom eyes me critically. "You can start by putting on one of those aprons." He points to a row of black vinyl aprons hanging from hooks on the wall. "They're waterproof. They'll keep your clothes dry, mostly."

I grab an apron and tie it on. "Okay. Show me what to do."

Tom proceeds to run me through the process. What goes where. How to clean what. He demonstrates putting a rack of dishes and bowls into the industrial dishwasher.

Casey brings in a tub of dirty dishes, which he sets on a stainless steel counter. "Chrissy told me you were the new dishwasher, but I didn't believe it. I still don't."

"Just try to keep up," Tom says as he nudges me with his elbow. "Casey will be bringing in dirty dishes as fast as you can wash them. Try not to fall behind."

"Thanks, Tom," I say as Casey walks away shaking his head. "I think I can manage."

It takes me about an hour to get the hang of the equipment. Casey keeps dumping tubs of dirty dishes on the counter. I sort and scrape and rinse everything, organizing it before the trays go into the washer.

I ignore the stares I'm getting from the two cooks—Jerome and Terry.

The two female servers keep peeking through the kitchen door at me. I guess they've never seen a former hitman washing dishes. I even catch Ruth once watching me through the kitchen order window.

At midnight, as soon as the last load of dishes is clean, I dry my hands, roll down my sleeves, and grab my jacket. I find Ruth behind the bar.

"All done for the night?" she asks, sounding very detached and matter-of-fact.

I nod. "Yeah. I guess I'll see you tomorrow at four."

"I guess so." She doesn't even make eye contact.

I stand there a full minute, hoping to get more of a reaction from her, anything, but she's busy making final drink orders. "Goodnight, Ruth. I guess I'll see you tomorrow." And I turn to walk away.

"Why did you come back, really?" she asks, practically blurting out the question.

I'd been waiting for that question all evening.

How the hell do I answer that?

Because I want you?

Because I need you?

Because I'm hoping you'll—what? Give me another chance?

In the end, I opt for honesty. "I came back here because I'm really hoping for a do-over with you."

She nods. "I guess I'll see you tomorrow then."

I've barely taken two steps before she asks, "Where are you staying?"

"I got a room at The Lone Wolf. It'll do until I find something a little more permanent."

She nods. I'm hoping she'll say more, but she doesn't. I certainly don't expect her to invite me to stay at her place. So I walk away, down the hallway and out the back door. I guess I should be grateful she's even talking to me after what I put her through.

She gave me a job—not the one I wanted, but it'll have to do for now.

* * *

The next few days pass without incident. I show up for work every day a few minutes before four, roll up my sleeves, and get to work washing dishes. Chrissy and Jess keep peeking in on me. Tom's keeping a close eye on me, and Ruth is studiously avoiding me.

Standing for eight hours, even on a padded mat, is harder than I realized. I'm used to being physically active, keeping on the move. I think I should trade my boots in for some proper industrial work shoes.

One time I glance over at the open kitchen door to find Micah staring at me. "Hey, Micah." I'm up to my elbows in hot, soapy water, so I can only nod. "How's it going?"

"Fine." He walks into the kitchen. "I had to see this with my own eyes. Word's getting around town that the big, bad mobster-killer is washing dishes at the tavern."

"Well, now I'm the big, bad dishwasher."

Shaking his head, Micah chuckles. "Seriously, I hope you know what you're doing."

"Yeah, so do I." I've been back three days now, and so far Ruth hasn't said more than a dozen words to me since that first night. Still, I've found her watching me a few times, either through the order window or through the open kitchen door. "Your sister is stubborn."

Micah laughs. "You think?"

Somehow I end up in charge of carrying the trash bags out to the dumpster behind the building. Late one night, as I'm lugging three bags out, I step out the back door to find Jess smoking a cigarette. "Hey, Jess." I set the bags on the ground beside the dumpster, then prop open the lid so I can drop them inside.

Jess drops her cigarette on the pavement and grounds out the embers with her bootheel. "So, how's it going, Jack?"

"I can't complain."

"I never figured I'd see you washing dishes for a living."

"What can I say? I need a job." Actually, I don't need a job. I've got enough money saved to last me a good long while. The rest of my life if I don't go too crazy. But what I really need is an excuse to be here every day, to see Ruth, be close to her. To breathe the same air she's breathing, and hope she—

"I live just over there," she says, nodding toward one of the apartment buildings a block over. She comes closer, stopping just inches away, and cranes her neck to meet my gaze, putting a whole lot of cleavage on display in the process. She looks up at me from beneath her long, dark lashes. "If you'd like to stop by after work, I'd love the company."

Well, this is awkward. "Jess, you're a very attractive woman—"

"But the answer's no?"

"Right. Sorry, but no." I'd clarify and say *hell no*, but there's no point in being rude.

Jess shrugs off my rejection like it's nothing. "I figured as much, but there's no harm in trying, right? It's not like you and Ruth are even talking to each other, let alone an item."

Biting my tongue, I slam the lid on the trash dumpster and head for the back door.

"Ruth is one lucky woman," she says as I pass by.

I glance back at Jess, but don't say anything. There's really nothing to say.

22

Ruth

I'm surprised to see Chris Nelson walk into the bar the next afternoon, dressed in his uniform. He takes his hat off as he approaches the bar. "Is Jack here?" he asks. "Rumor has it you've got him washin' dishes."

I can hear the disapproval in his voice. "Rumor would be correct, then," I say. And clearly everyone thinks that makes me the bad guy. I suppose they're right.

Chris snickers. "Well, at least he's not cleaning toilets."

"What do you want with Jack? I thought all the unpleasantness was behind us."

"Oh, you mean the mob? Yeah, that's old news, at least as far as I know. I'm here for something else entirely. Did you hear the McIntyre SAR team is out looking for a missing young woman today?"

"I heard. Micah's flying his chopper around the region so Killian can use infrared to search for her." I finish pouring some draft beers for Chrissy. "But what does that have to do with Jack?"

"I'd like to ask him if he'd mind helping out with this. Face it, Ruth. He's got some seriously bad-ass skills I could really use. The search and rescue mission has a certain urgency about it, and we need all the help we can get. Turns out the young woman is pregnant."

"Of course you can ask Jack. He's free to do whatever he wants, and knowing him, he'll want to help." I point behind me. "You'll find him in the kitchen."

"Thanks." He raises an eyebrow. "So, you've got a ten-year US Navy SEAL veteran in the kitchen washing dishes?"

My face heats up. "Well, when you put it like that."

With a chuckle, Chris waves me off. "I'm sure you have your reasons. I'll go have a talk with him. If he agrees, it's okay with you?"

"Sure. Tom and I can fill in for him."

"Please tell me you've posted a HELP WANTED ad."

"I have." I point Chris toward the kitchen. "Go talk to him."

I follow Chris and hover near the open doorway so I can listen in as he fills Jack in on the situation. Jack listens, nodding a few times. When Chris is done, Jack dries his hands on a kitchen towel, removes his work apron, and grabs his jacket. On his way out of the kitchen, he stops abruptly when he catches me lurking in the hall.

"Chris told me he filled you in. It's okay with you if I leave for a while?" he asks.

"Of course. Thanks for agreeing to help in the search."

Jack nods. "How can I say no? If I can be of any help, I will."

Of course he will, because he's a selfless helper. He's a hero. Suddenly I realize how much time I've wasted keeping Jack at arm's length, when I should have been pulling him closer. We might have gotten off to a rocky start, but obviously, he's a good guy. On impulse, I reach for his hand. "Just be careful, okay?"

I think my gesture caught him by surprise. He squeezes my hand. "Don't worry. I'll be fine."

"You'd better be, because there are things we need to

talk about when you get back."

He grins. "Yeah?"

I can't resist smiling back. "Yeah."

"It's a date," he says, giving my hand one last squeeze before he releases it and heads for the rear door.

My heart skips a beat as I watch him walk away, admiring his ass and his cocky stride. The urge to call him back is strong. If it weren't for the missing girl, I'd take him upstairs to my apartment right now so we could have that *talk*.

* * *

I watch from my office window as Jack, in his Impala, follows Chris's patrol vehicle out of the parking lot. I imagine they're headed to the trailhead, where the search and rescue teams congregate to organize and coordinate their efforts. This mission is probably child's play compared to the types of missions Jack's used to, but still, anything could go wrong.

When I return to the bar, Tom offers to do dish duty while Jack's gone.

"Thanks, Tom." I pat him on the back. "I appreciate you stepping in. I'll post some help-wanted flyers in the diner and grocery store. We need to get someone in to fill that job on a permanent basis."

Tom laughs. "So, you're done punishing Jack?"

"Is that what it looks like? That I'm punishing him?"

Tom frowns as he nods. "Afraid so."

The afternoon passes slowly, and I try not to worry about Jack. I hope they find that young woman quickly and that she's in good health.

Chrissy walks up to the bar to place a beer order. "Two drafts. I heard Jack's going out on a search and rescue mission."

I shake my head as I fill the first mug. "Word sure travels fast around here."

"Is it true?" she asks.

"Yes."

She sighs. "That man, sheesh! Can he get any hotter?" She chuckles. "Look, if you don't want him, do you mind giving the rest of us a shot?"

Hell yes, I mind.

"Here's your order," I say tersely, handing Chrissy two draft beers.

Wisely, she walks away with her order, not waiting for an answer.

23

Jack

I follow the sheriff's SUV to the Morrison Trailhead. This is where the girl's car was found earlier this morning after her co-workers reported her missing when she didn't show up to work at the Dairy Freeze. There are a couple dozen folks standing around the parking lot, grouped into smaller teams. A female deputy is presiding over a map spread out on the hood of her patrol car, a big black marker in hand as she draws and assigns search parameters to the various teams.

I pop open my trunk to access gear appropriate for wilderness tracking—camo pants, hiking boots, a weapons belt, and a camo armored tactical vest. I load the vest up with what I think I might need on an op like this—a flashlight, binoculars, zip ties, night vision goggles, a couple of water bottles and some protein bars, and a small emergency medical kit. The belt holds my Glock, spare magazines, and a knife.

Hannah McIntyre walks up beside me. "You look like you're going to war."

I shrug. "It pays to be prepared. We don't know what we'll run into up there."

She nods. "We have several former military personnel in our organization—Killian, Owen, John—all with extensive weapons training. They all carry. We try to make sure there's an experienced armed person on each team, as a precaution. You'll be paired with Maya and Travis. They're rock climbers by profession, not sharpshooters. So, I'm hoping you'll take point."

"Not a problem." I grab a can of bear spray and slip it into a vest pocket. "Are you expecting trouble?"

She winces. "We're not sure, but I think it's a distinct possibility. The girl's boyfriend is MIA. No one can find him, and that's a bit problematic. You'd think he'd be involved in the search, right? Worried about his girlfriend. But no. No one has seen him all day."

"That's certainly a bit of a red flag. Duly noted. Thanks for the heads-up."

"Officer Connelly—Stacy—will give you your search coordinates." She points to the deputy with the map and the marker. "Maya has a satellite phone. We ask all teams to report in to me on the hour."

I nod. "Got it."

As I slam my trunk lid down, she adds one thing more. "Be careful out there, Jack. Ruth will kill me if anything happens to you."

I chuckle at Hannah's words. "Got it."

Before we parted, Ruth told me we needed to talk when I get back. I'm trying not to let myself get too excited, or read too much into her words, but I'm hopeful.

"Here they are now," Hannah says as a guy and girl approach. "Jack, meet your teammates, Maya McKendrick and Travis Hicks."

The guy looks to be in his late twenties, the woman a few years younger. He's got brown hair and a trim brown beard, about six feet tall. The woman is stunning. Asian, with long black hair pulled back in a high ponytail, petite, dressed in ripped jeans and a blue-and-white plaid flannel shirt over a dark blue t-shirt. They're both dressed for serious hiking, along with packing ropes and carabiners.

I offer my hand to the guy, and we shake. "Travis. Nice to meet you." He's got a good, solid grip. When I offer my hand to the young woman, she frowns, but takes it anyway. Another good, solid grip. Well, of course, they're both rock climbers. They've got a lot of finger strength.

The guy seems pretty chill, laid back. But the girl? Based on the way she's glaring at me, she's got bad attitude written all over her. Hell, I haven't even said a word to her. I haven't even had time to piss her off.

I nod to their gear. "You two planning on doing some climbing?"

Travis shakes his head. "Not likely, but we might have to rappel into a ravine."

Hannah gestures across the parking lot to the deputy's cruiser. "You three go check in with Officer Connelly to get your search coordinates. Keep in touch out there."

We stop by the deputy's patrol car, and Officer Connelly gives us our coordinates.

"You're looking for Ashley Thompson," she tells us as she hands Maya a flyer with the missing girl's picture and physical description. "Twenty years old, curly blonde hair, and blue eyes. She's five foot five and weighs 140 pounds."

Maya folds the flyer and sticks it in her back pocket.

Now that we have our instructions, we hit the trail. We have a three-mile, uphill hike before we even reach our search zone.

Maya takes the lead, and we hit the trail at a brisk pace, walking single file to make room for the other search parties coming and going. Travis is next, and I take up the rear. I try not to show it, but I feel like I'm on babysitting duty. And lucky me, I got assigned to the cool kids.

The trail is a pretty steep incline, and soon my leg muscles are feeling the exertion. Thank God I've been hiking and running lately to acclimate myself to this elevation. Otherwise, I'd be hard pressed to keep up.

* * *

Even though the terrain is pretty steep, we still make decent time. Maya sets a grueling pace.

We reach our initial search coordinates in just under an hour. I'm not breathing too hard yet, which is a huge bonus. These two could probably run ten miles up this trail without breaking a sweat. But me? I'd be gasping for air.

When we finally split off the main trail, we walk deeper into the trees, heading south off the trail. I take over the lead position, and Maya and Travis follow behind.

"Ashley!" Maya yells. She's got a hell of an outdoor voice for such a petite woman.

"Ashley!" Travis calls.

I can hear other people off in the distance, shouting the girl's name. I have to chuckle to myself because the types of ops I'm used to are done in secrecy, in absolute silence. The upside to all the noise is, hopefully, it will scare off any black bears or other predators in the area.

I glance up at the sound of a helo passing by overhead.

"That's Micah," Maya says. "He and Killian are searching by air. Killian's using infrared goggles hoping to spot her heat signature."

Heat signature? I don't bother stating the obvious—that works only if the girl is still alive. I pick up the pace, scanning the terrain for signs that someone passed through here ahead of us.

At the top of the hour, Maya uses the satellite phone to report in to Hannah. "Nothing yet," she says.

Hannah thanks her for the update and signs off.

And we keep hiking.

The three of us spread out in a line, still within sight of each other, so we can cover more territory. I'm examining the ground, the soil, the brush, looking for signs that someone passed by this way.

We've been out here for two hours when we cross a slow-moving, shallow stream and I spot our first clue—shoe prints on the far muddy bank. Not just one pair, but two. I whistle sharply to signal the others, who hustle over to join me.

"What is it?" Travis asks. He glances down at the prints. "Shit."

Maya joins us and frowns as she stares at the ground. "*Two* sets of prints? What the hell?"

"This set of prints was made by a female wearing sneakers," I say, pointing to the impressions on the left. "This other set was made by a male wearing hiking boots. Call Hannah and confirm our search coordinates. We need to rule out the possibility we've crossed over into another team's designated territory. Let her know about the two sets of prints."

Maya gets Hannah on the sat phone. She confirms our coordinates and relays what we've found. "She says we're in the right place."

I start off in the direction of the prints. "Then it seems

Ashley's not alone up here." Unfortunately, the ground dries up within a few feet of the shoreline, and the prints are no longer visible.

"Assuming this is even Ashley," Travis says, "—and that's a big assumption—she either made a friend up here, or...."

I nod. "Or, we might have a problem on our hands."

Half an hour later, Hannah calls us back with an update. Maya puts the sat phone on speaker so we can all hear.

"I just spoke to Ashley's sister, Emily. Emily says last night Ashley had a big fight with her boyfriend over the pregnancy. Apparently, the boyfriend doesn't want anything to do with the baby, and Ashley insists on keeping it. And the boyfriend is still missing. Chris has put out an APB on him." She pauses. "So, guys, I'm wondering if the second set of foot prints you saw belong to him."

My gut tells me we're not looking for a missing hiker at all, but rather something more nefarious.

"You guys need to be careful up there," Hannah says.

"Understood," I reply.

We trudge through the woods another hour before I spot a small pop of fluorescent orange off in the distance beside a small stream. *Way to camouflage your where-*

abouts, dude.

I raise my hand, signaling to Travis and Maya to stop. "I think that's a pup tent," I say as I pull out my binoculars. "Yep. And I see one individual, a guy, early twenties, long brown ponytail, seated by a campfire. No one else. You two wait here while I go take a closer look. Stay out of sight until I determine if this guy's a threat or not."

Slowly, I make my way toward the campsite, circling around to the east to keep him from spotting me. When I approach, I come in from behind the tent so I can check it out before I make contact with the guy.

Quietly, I approach the small orange tent, which is zipped up tight. There's no sound coming from within, no movement. I don't see any indication there's someone in there.

The guy is seated in front of the fire with his back to me. I move around the tent, no longer bothering to be stealthy, so he hears me coming.

The guy, presumably Kyle, shoots to his feet and faces me. "Who the hell are you?" he says, scowling at me. "Where did you come from?"

"Hey, how's it going?" I ask casually, attempting to calm him down. "I was hiking and somehow I got off course. Can you point me toward the Morrison Trail?"

He looks doubtful. "You're pretty far-off track, man."

I glance around the area as if looking for a landmark. "I'm so turned around. Can you at least point me in the right direction?"

"No idea," he says. "And I don't give a fuck. Get lost."

That's when I hear it—the rustling of material coming from inside the tent, faint at first, then growing louder until it's clear that someone's thrashing.

The guy's eyes dart to the tent, then back to me. "I said go! Now!"

I raise my hands in a placating gesture. "Sure, man. No problem." I take a step closer. "I didn't mean to intrude."

When I hear muffled cries coming from inside the tent, I know the shit's about to hit the fan. The guy reaches back and pulls out a 9mm handgun. He points it right at me, his hand shaking. "I told you to go!"

"Okay. Calm down." *Damn it.* I really don't want to draw on this kid. "Who's in the tent, Kyle?" I ask, taking another step toward him. I need to get in striking distance.

His eyes widen as he realizes I know who he is. Which means I also know who's in the tent. "It wouldn't happen to be Ashley Thompson, would it?"

The guy's hand is shaking so badly right now I don't

think he could hit the broad side of a barn if he tried. I take another step closer and hold out my nondominant hand. "Give me the gun, Kyle."

My dominant hand is ready to draw on him if he so much as breathes wrong.

Kyle shakes his head. "I don't know what the hell you're talking about."

"Be careful where you point that thing. You might shoot somebody."

"Starting with you," he says.

I laugh, which throws him off guard, and take another step closer. "I don't think so." Now that I'm within reach, I strike out, grasp both his wrist and the gun, twist, and wrench the weapon out of his hand.

He cries out in pain, cradling his wrist.

"Oh, come on," I say. "I didn't even break it." I tuck his handgun into the back waistband of my weapons belt and pull out a zip tie. I've got his wrists pinned behind his back and secured before he knows what hit him.

I whistle to Maya and Travis, signaling that the coast is clear.

When I unzip the tent door, I find a young woman with curly blonde hair and big, tear-filled blue eyes staring up at me, her expression a mix of terror and relief.

She's lying on top of a sleeping bag, both her ankles and wrists tied with duct tape. There's also a strip of tape over her mouth. "Ashley, right?"

She nods enthusiastically, murmuring incoherently from behind the tape.

As soon as I cut Ashley free, she crawls out of the tent and throws herself at me, her arms going around my waist. "Thank you," she sobs over and over. "Thank you."

I glance over at Kyle, who's sitting by the fire. "You really didn't think this through, did you, Kyle?"

He glares at me. "Fuck you."

When Maya and Travis join us, she calls Hannah to let her know we found Ashley safe and sound. We also fill her in on Kyle's presence.

Hannah hands the phone over to Chris on their end, and we fill him in on the details. He tells me that Micah's on his way with the chopper to pick up Kyle. Killian will take Kyle into custody and deliver him to the sheriff.

Travis checks Ashley over to make sure she's not injured. I offer her a bottle of water and one of my protein bars.

"I don't want to ride with Kyle," Ashley says as she scarfs down the protein bar. She takes a long swig of water. "Can I walk out with you guys? I feel fine, I swear.

I really can't face looking at Kyle one more minute."

It's not a difficult hike, just a bit tiring.

"Sure," I say. "If that's what you want. You can take twenty minutes to get off this mountain via helicopter, or you can spend three to four hours hiking out. It's your choice."

She smiles. "At least it's all downhill, right?"

* * *

Micah sets the helo down in an open area about three hundred feet from the campsite where we're waiting. Killian comes to assess the situation. He talks to Ashley, making sure she's okay. He tries to talk her into riding back with them on the chopper, but she's adamant that she wants to walk. Since she seems physically fine, Killian okays her request.

Killian handcuffs Kyle and marches him to the helicopter.

Travis and I pack up all of Kyle's camping gear to bring down with us. Then the four of us start our hike back to the trailhead.

When we reach the trail and start our trek down to the parking lot, we're joined by other searchers who have come to congratulate us. By the time we reach the parking lot, we've amassed quite a group.

Chris Nelson comes to shake my hand. "Good work," he tells me. "Not a single shot fired."

"Kyle was terrified. I was pretty sure he wouldn't shoot me." I remove Kyle's handgun from my waistband and hand it over to the sheriff. "Evidence."

Chris nods. "Thanks. By the way, Jack, if you're interested, I've got an opening in my department with your name on it. Have you ever considered a career in law enforcement?"

I chuckle. "Thanks, but I'll have to pass. I've got a cushy job right now as a dishwasher. Why mess up a good thing?"

Maya bumps elbows with me. "Hey, you'd look good in a uniform, especially for a guy your age."

"My age? Gee, thanks, Maya. I'll keep that in mind." And then to Chris, I say, "If I'm done here, there's someone I need to go see."

Chris grins. "Really? I think I can guess who." He pats my shoulder. "Good luck, pal."

24

Ruth

Around eight o'clock, the McIntyre search and rescue team members start arriving at the bar to celebrate the win. Not only did they *find* a missing pregnant hiker, but they *rescued* her from her abductor. Or rather, I should say, *Jack* rescued her. I heard all about how he took down the girl's armed boyfriend single-handedly, without even drawing his own weapon.

Of course he did. Does that guy even know how *not* to be a hero?

When Killian and Hannah walk in, along with the sheriff and several deputies, the customers applaud. Word's already gotten around town that Ashley is home safe tonight with her parents.

Maya and Travis walk in next, followed shortly after by John Burke and his girlfriend, Gabrielle. When Micah arrives, he's immediately swamped by a wave of single girls.

Jack is the last to arrive. When he walks in through the back hallway, the customers in the bar take note, stand, and applaud.

"Wow, a standing ovation," I say to Jack, as I clap along with everyone else. "Impressive."

Jack shrugs. "Hey, I was just doin' my job. No big deal."

I'm standing behind the bar when Jack takes a seat opposite me. He looks freshly showered. The ends of his hair are still damp and curling, and he smells amazing, like soap, fresh laundry, and a hint of cologne.

"Chris offered me a job," he says.

My heart skips a beat. "Oh?" Suddenly, my chest tightens at the thought of him leaving to work somewhere else.

"Yeah. In law enforcement. What do you think of that? Me, a deputy?" He chuckles.

I can't tell if he's seriously considering the offer or not. It would make perfect sense for him to go into law enforcement. It would be good, steady work in a worthwhile field. He has an excellent set of skills that would serve him well, and the rest he would learn quickly.

"Chris would be lucky to have you," I admit. "What did you tell him?"

Jack shrugs. "I told him thanks, but no thanks. I've already got a great gig here as a dishwasher."

That's it. I can't take this anymore. I walk out from behind the bar, and nod toward the back hallway. "Can I talk to you? In private?"

"Sure," he says as he stands. Grinning, he follows me.

I lead him into my office and shut the door behind us. After taking a slow, steadying breath, I turn to face him, my hands on my hips. My pulse is racing, and I realize I'm nervous. What if he says *no*? Damn it, I should have done this as soon as he returned to Bryce. "If you're still interested—"

"I am."

"Wait." I bite back a laugh. "You didn't let me finish."

"I don't need to. The answer is yes."

When he takes a step toward me, I raise my hand to hold him off. "Let me say this, Jack, please."

"Okay." He crosses his arms over his chest, still grinning. "I'm all ears."

"If you're still interested," I begin, "I could use another bartender. The position's yours, if you still want it. I'm sorry about the dishwashing—"

"Stop." He steps closer and cups my face. "You don't need to apologize."

"Yes, I do. I was an ass for making you do the dishes."

Still grinning, he says, "True. But it's fine. It's honest work. No one's above doing honest work." His gaze fixes on mine as he holds out his hand.

I give him my hand, but instead of shaking it, he holds it securely in both of his. His gaze darkens as he searches mine. There's no resentment there, just anticipation.

"I wasn't expecting you to come back here," I say, "but I'm glad you did. What are you going to do about accommodations? You can't live in the motel indefinitely. It's too expensive."

He shrugs. "I'll get an apartment in town. Eventually, I might want to buy a house or purchase some land and build. I'll just have to wait and see how things go." *With you.* He doesn't say that part, but it's implied.

Sighing, I say, "You're welcome to use the apartment upstairs until you decide what you want to do in the long term. If you want to, that is. You don't have to."

He looks like he just won the lottery. "Really? I can use your place?"

"Sure. It's yours for as long as you want it." I walk over to my desk, open the top drawer, and pull out a keychain with two keys. "The silver one is for the back door, so you can get into the building. And this gold key is for the apartment." I hand him the keychain, and he pockets it.

The way he's looking at me, I fully expect him to kiss me any second now. We haven't kissed, or even touched each other, since the night we spent together in the upstairs apartment. I wonder if he's thinking the same thing. The hunger in his eyes tells me he is.

Jack takes a step toward me, and then stops, hesitating.

I try not to let my disappointment show. I guess if I was hoping we could simply pick up where we left off, I was wrong. I hurt him when I pushed him away after that first night together.

I take a step toward him, closing the distance between us. "I owe you an apology. I've been burned so many times, I've become afraid to take any more chances. It's just easier going it alone."

He frowns. "You were taking chances on the wrong guys, Ruth. You should have waited for me because I'm a good bet."

I can't help smiling. "I'm starting to think you're right."

He cups my face and looks into my eyes, his own reflecting so much vulnerability. I realize he's taking a risk here, too. It's not just me.

When he leans in, I close my eyes and practically hold my breath. I want this to work so badly. I want him to be the one.

Slowly, he lowers his mouth to mine and gently nudges my lips open. His hands slide down to my shoulders, then down my arms, gripping them firmly. I feel a delicious tug all the way to my very core, leaving me quivering with anticipation. My body heats, and soon I'm a hot, aching mess.

When there's a knock at the door, Jack pulls back with a groan and stares at the door. "That is the very definition of bad timing."

"Sorry for the interruption, Ruth," Tom says, his voice muffled by the door. "It's getting pretty intense out here. We're almost near capacity. I could really use another pair of hands behind the bar."

Jack presses a quick kiss to my lips. "I guess now would be a good time for me to start my new job." He nods toward the door. "You'd better come teach me the basics."

I let him take my hand and pull me along with him to the door. "I guess so," I say with a stupid smile on my face as we walk back to the bar, hand in hand.

* * *

The place is packed all night long, thanks to all the buzz and excitement around town. The success of the search and rescue mission is all over the evening news; even the national networks and cable news programs are picking it up. A lot of our customers are gathered around the only TV in the place. I guess people are interested in the story of the poor pregnant girl who was kidnapped by her boyfriend.

Most of the extra bodies in the bar are here out of curiosity. They want to meet the search and rescue team. Jack, himself, gets a lot of the attention, although he tries to deflect it.

He and I work the bar together, side by side, as I basically walk him through what I do. I hand him my spiral-bound, handmade cocktail recipe book for him to use as a reference.

But honestly, most of the orders are for bottles of beer, mugs of draft beer, straight shots, and soft drinks.

It's not hard. While he takes care of the easy orders, I mix the cocktails, while Tom handles the dirty dishes.

Jack takes to bartending like a natural, smiling and joking with customers. He has a friendly, easygoing way about him that I lack. I'm an introvert, but clearly he's not.

It doesn't escape my notice that most of the people asking for drinks at the bar are single women of all ages, from just barely twenty-one to women in their forties and fifties. I can't blame them. He is pretty nice to look at. Okay, better than nice if I'm being honest. Panty melting is a better description. And his deep voice! God, his voice makes me weak in the knees. His voice belongs in our deepest, darkest, sexiest dreams.

Around nine, the hype seems to have dissipated. Most of the onlookers have left, and things have settled down to more normal levels.

Hannah and Killian and the rest of the SAR team, including my brother, have commandeered a couple of tables and are having a proper celebration.

I hear a cheer go up when Maggie and her husband, Owen, walk in. Owen's got their baby daughter, Claire, propped on his hip. Her light brown hair has turned curly, like her mama's, and she's got her dad's blue eyes.

Maya jumps up from the table and makes a beeline for the baby, holding out her hands and stealing Claire away from her doting father.

Owen walks up to the bar and shakes Jack's hand. "Good work today."

Killian joins them. "I hope you'll consider my offer to join the team," he says to Jack. "We can really use someone with your skills."

Jack nods to me. "Sure. If my new boss will let me have the time off work."

I bump Jack's shoulder with my own. "Of course, you can do whatever you want with your time."

"I think that's a yes, then," Jack says to Killian. "Count me in."

Micah walks up to the bar, having heard the tail end of their conversation. "Kudos to you for getting him to say yes," he says to Killian. "Chris offered him a job with the police department, but Jack turned him down."

Maggie and Owen don't stay long, as it's already way past Claire's bedtime. The baby's losing steam, sucking her thumb as she lays her head on Maggie's shoulder.

The rest of the team call it a night and file out through the back door, leaving us with our typical late-night clientele.

A phone call comes in on the landline. Turns out it's someone responding to my HELP WANTED flyer for a dishwasher. His name is Scott, and he just moved back to Bryce and is desperate for a job. The good news is he has two years experience in operating commercial kitchen dishwashers. I invite the guy to come in tomorrow for an interview, and if everything checks out okay, he can start right away. Tom will certainly be happy to hear that.

"It looks like we might have a new dishwasher soon," I say, crossing my fingers.

"Good," Jack says. "I thought my fingers were going to turn into prunes."

That night, at closing time, I offer to let Tom go home while Jack and I lock up.

During a brief lull in the evening, Jack returned to The Lone Wolf, packed up his few belongings, and checked out of his motel room for good.

"So, you're all set then?" I ask Jack as I'm about to leave for the night. "Feel free to stock the apartment fridge tomorrow. Until then, if you need anything, you can help yourself to whatever you want in the kitchen or storeroom."

"I will. Do you mind if I purchase a few things for the

apartment? Not a lot, just a few necessities."

"Go right ahead," I say.

When we're done with all the closing chores, Jack walks me to the rear door. I need to go home, and there's no reason for me to stay, but I hate the idea of leaving.

"If you need anything, just let me know. About the apartment, I mean."

He nods. "Is there Wi-Fi up there?"

"Yes. The password is hank1960."

"I might get a TV—nothing big. Just something to stream movies on."

"Go right ahead." It's after one a.m., and I should be going. "I guess I'll see you tomorrow then."

This is ridiculous. We're both standing here like awkward teens who don't know what to do at the end of the night.

Jack reaches out and touches my cheek. "Goodnight, Ruth."

"Goodnight, Jack."

After I let myself out, Jack stands in the open doorway and watches me get into my Jeep and start the engine. As I pull away, I see the door finally close.

All the way home, I fight the urge to go back. I want to bridge the distance that has grown between us, but I don't know how to. I really wish we could just start over.

25

Jack

The next morning, I shower, dress, and head to Maggie's. When I walk into the grocery store, I find her standing at the check-out counter. Her baby is asleep in some kind of baby sling strapped to Maggie's chest. I notice the back door is propped open, and Owen is wheeling in a dolly stacked high with boxes. I can hear a big truck idling out back.

"Good morning," I say. "Claire, right? I saw you bring her into the bar last night. She's a beautiful baby."

"Thank you." Maggie smiles as she glances down at her daughter. She lightly fingers her soft, brown curls.

"Is she your first?" I ask.

"No. I have two teenagers, both boys. Their dad and I divorced years ago. I only recently met Owen, through Hannah McIntyre. Claire was sort of a surprise for both of us—but a welcome one. Do you like kids, Jack? Do you see yourself becoming a father one day?"

"I hope so. Time will tell, right?" I find it interesting that Maggie and her husband are around my age, and they have a baby. I guess there's still hope for me.

"So, what brings you in this morning?" she asks.

"I have a kitchen to stock. I'll be staying in the apartment above the bar for the foreseeable future, and right now the fridge is empty."

"You've come to the right place," she says. "Let me know if you need help finding anything."

I grab a cart and start filling it with everything a person needs on a daily basis, everything from toilet paper to bread and butter, eggs, pop and beer. When I think I have the basics, I return to the check-out counter, and Maggie rings me up.

She winces. "Ouch. That'll be $210.59. Sorry."

"It's expensive to start from scratch, isn't it?"

Just as she's done counting out the cash I handed her, Owen walks up beside her and kisses her left temple. "That's everything. I'll take Claire home now and put her down for her morning nap. We'll come back later this afternoon, and I'll unpack and shelve everything."

"Thanks, honey," Maggie says.

"Can I help you haul that out to your car?" Owen asks me. We'd met briefly the day of the search and rescue mission. He's a good guy. Former military, I can tell. He's big, muscular, knows how to handle himself. It's clear he's crazy about his wife and baby.

"Actually, all this is going into the apartment above the bar," Maggie says. "Jack's moving in there."

Owen's eyes widen in surprise. "Really?" He glances at Maggie, a clear question in his eyes. "I can help you carry all this stuff up there if you like," he offers. "Maybe between the two of us, we can make it in two trips."

I don't mind making the extra trips, and I don't really need help, but I figure this is a good opportunity to get to know Owen better. "That'd be great, if you have the time. Thanks."

"No problem," Owen says, brushing off my thanks. "I'd be happy to."

After we carry all the groceries up to the apartment,

Owen leaves, and I unpack everything and put the stuff away.

Now I can move on with the rest of today's agenda. I plan to stop in at the diner for lunch—namely to visit Jenny Lopez. After that, I'll stop in at Micah's auto repair shop and have a chat with him. My tires need rotating, I'm sure of it.

I figure by spending time with Ruth's friends, I'll make a good impression and learn more about her in the process. I'm not above mining her friends for intel. It's all part of my diabolical plan to convince her I'm the right guy for her.

I head to the diner for lunch—a turkey melt with fries and hot apple pie with vanilla ice cream. I'm seated at the counter, so Jenny has lots of opportunities to chat with me between waiting on customers and dishing out more pie. She's one hell of a multitasker, and she keeps that diner running smoothly with a pretty small support staff.

"So, Jenny," I say after taking a sip of coffee, "what do you think Ruth would consider the perfect date?"

Jenny grins. "Smart man. Anything outdoors. She loves hiking, and she loves water. You could even take her fishing. Her grandpa always took Ruth and Micah fishing when they were young. Kayaking is also good. Canoeing."

"What about whitewater rafting? I hear there's some good rafting around here."

Jenny shakes her head. "No, that's too chaotic and noisy for Ruth. She likes quiet. She's an introvert, if you hadn't noticed."

I smile. "Yeah, I've noticed. Okay, hiking and water. Got it."

Jenny raises her index finger. "Oh, and good food. She likes food. She likes to try new restaurants, but with working so many hours, she doesn't have a lot of time for that. Make time for it. Take her to Estes Park or Boulder or Fort Collins. There's even Denver, of course, although that's a bit of a drive. Ruth works long and hard and rarely takes time off for herself. She needs someone who will coax her into taking time to have fun. But don't baby her. She doesn't want to be coddled. She's independent to the core. The right man for her will understand that and give her space. Respect her strengths."

"Thanks, Jenny. I appreciate the info."

Jenny reaches out and squeezes my hand. "I'm glad you're here. Ruth is amazing, and she deserves someone equally amazing. I think that's you. You just have to learn how to break through her protective walls without breaking her in the process."

After I leave the diner, I head to Micah's auto shop. I walk into the office to speak to the woman sitting at the front desk. She's reading a dog-eared romance paperback. "Is Micah here?"

"In the shop," she says without taking her eyes off her book. She points behind her at a glass door.

Through the door, I can see Micah leaning over the engine of a silver minivan. "Thanks." I join Micah beside the vehicle and gaze down at the engine. "Hey."

He glances up at me. "You're still here? What do you want?"

Ouch. Tough crowd. But he's her brother, so I shouldn't expect anything different. He's just watching out for his sister. I get it. "Yeah, I'm still here. I plan to be here for a while. Hopefully a good long while."

Micah frowns. "What does that mean?"

"It means that I came back to Bryce for Ruth. Your sister is an amazing woman, Micah, and I want to be part of her life."

Micah straightens and studies me for a moment. Then he nods. "I can't disagree with your assessment of my sister. So, what do you want with me?"

"I want us to get to know one another. I'm hoping we can be friends because I can use all the allies I can get."

He chuckles. "And you think I can help you with that?"

I nod. "Yeah, I'm hoping you can. You know Ruth better than anyone. What does she need in a partner?"

"My sister is strong-willed, ornery, and stubborn as hell. If you want to impress her, just don't get in her way. She's self-sufficient and fearless. Hell, she chops her own firewood for the wood stove when she could easily buy it and have it delivered. I've offered to chop it for her, and she gets pissy with me. Don't offer to chop her firewood, and don't kill the spiders for her. She can fend for herself. She doesn't *need* a man. So you have to make her *want* one. You have to show her you can add to her quality of life without taking away from it. Got it?"

"Yes, thanks. By the way, I need to make an appointment to get my tires rotated."

He raises an eyebrow. "Are you just trying to suck up to me by giving me business?"

I grin. "Yeah. Is it working?"

* * *

Scott, the new dishwasher shows up the next day for

his interview and he passes with flying colors. Ruth puts him straight to work, which makes everyone happy.

I work the bar that afternoon and evening, and at the end of the day, I take Ruth's cocktail recipe book back to the apartment with me to study it.

The next day, I make a trip to Estes Park to shop for a few furnishings I need for the apartment. Not much, but a few things for the kitchen and living room. I stop at one of those big box stores that carries everything and buy some books, a TV, pillows and a blanket for the sofa, cookware and a set of dishes and silverware. I don't know how Ruth makes do in that apartment, but it's lacking in pretty much everything.

That night, Ruth and I lock up after everyone else has gone home. She reconciles the till, while I turn off the OPEN sign and lock the front door.

When she's done, I walk her to the back door.

"Have you got everything you need?" she asks me.

"Actually, there's only one thing I need," I say.

The heat I see in her eyes is encouraging. "And what's that?"

I reach for her hand. "*You.* I need you." She lets me pull her into my arms. "Stay with me tonight," I say. "Let's have a sleepover."

"A sleepover?" she asks, smiling.

"Yeah. No sex, purely platonic. I just want to spend some time with you. Come on, I'll even make you some dinner. Neither one of us had a chance to grab anything to eat this evening. You've got to be hungry. Say yes, Ruth."

26

Ruth

I've never felt so nervous at the thought of being with someone. I'm not afraid to admit it. I want him in my life. These last few days have shown me sides of Jack I didn't see before. He's a good guy, with a good heart. I find myself drawn to him, *wanting him.* But the fantasy of him is one thing; reality is another. I thought I was making good choices in the past, and I was wrong.

I glance toward the rear exit—my escape—and then at the door leading upstairs. "Fine," I say with a heavy sigh. "I'll stay."

He laughs. "Try not to sound so enthusiastic. You'll give me a big head." And then he chuckles at his own double *entendre*.

I smile brightly and speak in a simpering, fake voice. "Yes, Jack, I'd love to spend the night with you. Nothing would make me happier."

"Hey, I get it," he says as he pulls me toward the door that leads upstairs. "You've been let down before and you're afraid it will happen again, but I'm telling you it won't. The first time we slept together wasn't a one-time thing, Ruth. Well, it was twice, but let's not get too technical. I'm here for the long haul. I came back to Bryce *for you*. Yes, the scenery here is pretty spectacular, the hiking is great, but the town itself is definitely lacking in amenities. I had to drive all the way to Estes Park just to find a laundromat."

I realize I'm smiling. This man always makes me smile. If he's willing to take a chance on me, I need to have the courage to return the favor. On impulse, I lean in and give him a peck on the lips. "Let's go upstairs."

He lets me into the apartment, and when I walk in, I'm taken aback. My barebones, utilitarian apartment actually has some character now. There are throw pillows and a blanket on the sofa. There are books on the coffee table, along with a laptop. The table's set with matching placemats, plates, and silverware. That's all new. He's making this apartment his *home*.

"I hope you don't mind," he says.

"No, it looks great."

"I stocked the fridge and pantry, too." He opens the fridge door to reveal a fully-stocked interior. "How about nachos? I make good nachos. There aren't a lot of meals I make well, but that's one of them. I'm also killer with a grill—burgers, steak, chicken. How about it? I even have some Corona to go along with dinner. I thought maybe we could eat and talk. Or, if you prefer, we could watch something together." He points to a TV sitting on a console across from the sofa.

"That's new," I say.

"It's only temporary, you know. I'll get my own place eventually and take it all with me."

"No, it's fine. The place looks great. It finally looks like someone lives here." I chuckle, feeling stupid. "I guess I assumed you asked me up here to have sex. Not for dinner and a show."

"Well, I thought, since we're starting over, this is technically our first date, and I'll have you know I don't have sex on the first date."

He says that last line with such a straight face, I burst into laughter.

"I thought, for tonight," he says, "we could eat and talk, you know? Get to know each other better. I was thinking we could have a sleepover—platonic, of course—and in the morning, we could drive to Estes Park for brunch. I found a great little breakfast café in town that makes killer pancakes, and their coffee is amazing. We could be back in Bryce in time to open the bar. How about it? A legitimate date."

"You've obviously put a lot of thought into this plan of yours."

He nods. "I didn't want you to think I was after you just for sex."

"If it was just sex, you could have your pick of probably any single girl in town, many of them much younger than me. Even half my age." I walk up to him and kiss him lightly on the lips. "I love your plan."

The smile he gives me makes my heart race.

He ushers me to one of the barstools at the kitchen counter. "Have a seat while I make you dinner."

He grabs a bottle of Corona from the fridge. "Want one?"

"Sure."

He opens it and hands it to me.

I sit on a barstool at the kitchen counter and watch as Jack makes nachos. I'm impressed that he actually knows what he's doing, browning ground beef and seasoning it with an impressive array of Mexican spices. He heats up refried beans, and layers both the beef and beans over a bed of restaurant style tortilla chips placed on a wide platter. He covers it all with a mix of shredded Mexican cheeses and sliced jalapeno peppers. He places the platter on the dining table, along with a bowl of sour cream and some fresh salsa.

And for a finishing touch, he lights a single candle in the center of the table.

I take a bite and groan in appreciation. "This is delicious."

"You sound surprised."

"I guess I am. I personally don't know a lot of men who can cook. Killian can, and Owen can, but that's about it. My brother would starve without take-out and microwaveable meals."

"I'm not just another pretty face, you know," he says. "I do know how to treat a woman. And just wait until brunch tomorrow. Those pancakes are—" He makes a chef's kiss.

As we eat, I finally have a chance to ask him something I've been wondering about. "So, tell me about your family."

"There's not much to tell, really," he says as he picks up a chip. "My parents are retired high school history teachers living in St. Augustine, Florida. I have one sibling, a sister, Carrie. She and her husband, Mark, live near our parents. They've got two young kids, a girl and a boy."

"What do they do? Your sister and her husband?"

"She's an obstetrician, and he's a pediatrician."

I laugh. "That's convenient. Do you see them often?"

He frowns as he shakes his head. "I'm ashamed to say no. When I was working in my last job, I didn't feel it was appropriate to be around them. I couldn't exactly tell them what I did for a living, could I?"

"Maybe now that you're in a new line of work, it would be a good time for you to pay them a visit."

He takes a swig of his beer. "Maybe you're right. I haven't even seen the newest baby yet. I'd say we're overdue for a family reunion. What about your family?"

I shrug. "You've already met my brother."

"Yeah, but what about your parents? And who's Hank?"

I smile. "Hank is—*was*—my paternal grandfather. He

built the bar back in the '60s."

"And your parents?" he asks.

"Our parents met in college—they were both architecture students at University of Colorado Denver. It was love at first sight, and they were married within a year. Our mom had me pretty quickly, and Micah was born when I was twelve. I think he might have been a surprise." I reach for a chip and chew for a minute. The next part still hurts to talk about.

"Our mom died in a car accident shortly after Micah was born. A distracted driver crossed the center line and hit her car head on. Dad was devastated. I don't think he ever fully recovered after losing her. We were living in Denver at the time. After Mom died, our dad moved us here to Bryce, to be close to his parents. We ended up living with them because our father traveled so frequently on business, and our grandparents pretty much raised us."

"You were close to your dad's parents."

"Very close. When Grandma died, I took over raising Micah, while Grandpa ran the tavern. When he passed, he left me the tavern and the cabin, and he left Micah money, which he used to open his car repair shop and buy a used helicopter." I take a swig of my beer.

"And your dad?"

"He lives in Vancouver, working as an architect."

"Did he ever remarry?"

"No. I don't think he ever will. Now, that's enough about me. Here." I pick up a loaded chip off the platter and offer it to him. His gaze darkens as he opens his mouth wide, and I slide it in.

After we eat, he shoos me to the sofa to sit and relax while he cleans up the kitchen and washes our few dishes. I offer to help, but he tells me no. He says he has professional dishwashing experience, which makes me laugh.

I can't remember the last time someone made me laugh so much.

When Jack's done in the kitchen, he dries his hands and joins me on the sofa.

It's two a.m., and I'm starting to run out of steam.

"I was going to suggest we watch a movie," he says, "but it's too late for that. Especially if we want to get up and go out for brunch in the morning." He stands and offers me his hand. "Let's go to bed."

"I thought we weren't having sex tonight."

"We aren't. But that doesn't mean we can't get comfortable in bed and cuddle. There's something I want to talk to you about, and it's probably best done under the cover of darkness."

"Okay, now you've got me worried."

He pulls me to my feet and steers me toward the bedroom.

* * *

I walk into the bathroom to find men's products everywhere—shaving cream, deodorant, men's shampoo in the shower and a bar of men's soap. I am deep into men's territory now.

After we wash up and brush our teeth, we change into pajamas. For Jack, that means a pair of black boxer briefs. He gives me one of his oversized US Navy T-shirts to wear to bed. We turn off the lights and climb into bed.

He lies on his back and pulls me close so that my head is resting on his shoulder. Automatically, he starts rubbing my back.

"So, what did you want to talk about?" I ask, hoping to get this over with quickly.

He's quiet for a while, just rubbing my back. Sometimes he slips his hand up underneath my braid and grips my neck, squeezing gently and sending tingles down my spine. I'm realizing how much he loves simple touches. He sighs heavily. "All right. Here goes. I want you to tell me about your marriage."

I flinch at the question. "My marriage? Why in the world do you want to hear about that?" I start to pull away, but he tugs me back.

"I'll tell you why," he says as he resumes rubbing my back. "Because it didn't work out, and I want to know why so I won't make the same mistake *he* did. What was his name?"

I blow out a long breath. "I don't even know where to start." I find myself drawing circles on his bare chest with the tip of my index finger as I contemplate whether—and even how—I can explain my failed marriage. I draw light circles around his nipples.

He lightly taps my ass. "Stop trying to distract me, Ruth. This is important."

"Fine, but there's not much to tell. It started out fine." I continue drawing shapes and figures on his chest, figure eights, curlicues. "We got along really well."

"What's his name?"

"Andy Brewer."

"Ok, and then what?"

"About a year into the marriage, he started making

off-handed comments about me working. He said he wanted me to stay home and be a housewife. I said no. I told him I loved my job. Hell, it's *my* bar. I wanted to run it. I *enjoyed* running it. We'd already talked about having kids—we were both in agreement on that. And he said that was even more reason why I should stop working. He said I should let Tom manage the bar for me. He even suggested I sell the bar. We fought over it, argued, so many times. This topic never came up when we were dating, or before we got married. Then all of a sudden, it took center stage in our life. It affected everything."

"He lied to you," Jack says. He slips his warm hand up underneath my T-shirt and skims it up and down my bare back, giving me goosebumps. "He knew if he told you upfront how he felt about you working that you wouldn't marry him. So, he waited until after you'd said your vows to bring it up. He hoped that, by then, it would be too late for you to back out."

"This went on for nearly two years," I continued. "We went to marriage counseling, but it soon became clear to me he wasn't going to let up on this. And neither was I. I wasn't going to give up the bar. I sure as hell wasn't going to sell it. We were at an impasse, so I filed for divorce."

"I'm sorry." He leans over and presses a kiss to my

forehead. "But I'm also grateful because it means I get a chance."

"How do you feel about kids?" I ask him, finally having the courage to broach the subject. If we're going to talk about big issues, then having kids is definitely one of the biggest.

"Do I want them? Yes." He's quiet a moment, and then he finally says, "I'd consider myself incredibly fortunate to become a father at my advanced age, after the life I've lived."

I laugh. "You're forty, Jack, not a doddering old man. Besides, men don't have biological clocks. Not the same way women do."

He tightens his arms around me. "My sister had her first baby at forty and another at forty-two, so it's possible. Do you want kids?"

"I do. I wish I'd started sooner, but yeah, I do. But then, I hadn't met the right guy yet, so I guess that's irrelevant."

He tightens his hold on me. "I'd love to make a baby with you. A little dark-haired, dark-eyed baby. I don't care what we have or how many. I just want to share my life with you."

"Don't you think we're jumping the gun here by talking about babies? Technically, this is our first date.

You said so yourself."

He leans over to kiss me. "Tomorrow's brunch will count as our second date. Will that be soon enough?"

I smile against his lips. "Maybe we should wait a few months before we have this conversation."

"Fine." He gazes at me, so intently, all his attention focused on me. "Do you believe in love at first sight? That you can meet someone and just *know* they're the one? When you look at them, your heart stops. Time stands still. I suppose you think that's sappy."

I chuckle. "It is a bit melodramatic, but yes, I actually do. My parents fell in love the moment they met in class. He said he walked into the room, saw her sitting in her seat, and he took the chair next to hers. He asked her to have coffee with him after class. He proposed a month later. They were very happy together for fifteen years."

Jack rolls us so that he's lying on top of me. He slides one of his legs between mine. "Time stood still for me the first moment I laid eyes on you. You were wearing blue jeans and a red-and-white flannel shirt. And when you took my first drink order, I was smitten." He slips his hand beneath the front of my T-shirt and cups one of my breasts, gently kneading it.

I stifle a groan. "I thought we weren't having sex

tonight."

"That was the plan."

I chuckle. "But things have changed?"

"I don't know," he says, his voice rough. "You tell me." He tugs my shirt up, exposing my breasts, and draws one of my nipples into his mouth and gently sucks.

Pleasure streaks through my body, all the way down to the heated spot between my legs. That part of me is suddenly aching.

I grab his hand and move it down my body, to between my legs, where I know he will feel my heat and arousal. "The plan has definitely changed, Jack."

That's all the invitation he needs. He rolls off me and tugs my T-shirt off. Then he proceeds to kiss his way down my body, starting with my forehead. He peppers kisses down my cheeks, my throat, until he reaches my breasts, which he pays especially close attention to.

When he skims his lips down my torso, my belly starts quivering. He keeps going, jacking up my arousal in the process. Finally, he moves down the bed and settles between my thighs, making himself right at home.

He peers up at me. "I've been thinking about this ever since I got back, wanting my mouth on you."

All I can do is grasp his thick hair and tug when his

tongue and fingers turn me into a hot mess. He's relentless and determined, reducing me to sharp cries as my orgasm hits me with little warning.

While I'm struggling to catch my breath, he shucks off his boxers and reaches into the nightstand drawer for a condom. Kneeling between my shaking thighs, he sheaths himself quickly, then leans over me as he guides himself to my opening.

Slowly, an inch at a time, he pushes inside me until he's fully seated. His gaze locks on mine, his eyes communicating *everything* he's feeling as my body softens for him. He moves slowly at first, pulling nearly all the way out before sliding in deep.

I slide my hands up his torso, dragging my nails over his taut skin. He's so tense, his rock-hard biceps bulging as he supports his weight. I slip my fingers into his hair and pull his mouth down to mine. Our lips cling, our tongues stroke and tease.

He's thrusting hard now, powering into me. My thighs are still shaking from my earlier climax. He thrusts one last time, deep, and holds himself there as his body shudders wildly. I can feel him throbbing inside me as he comes hard, his chest heaving as he tries to catch his breath.

Finally, he rolls us onto our sides, still joined, and brushes my hair back from my damp face. Then he cups my face and leans in to kiss me, his lips gentle, so reverent he makes my chest ache.

"All I ask," he says, "is that you give me a chance. Let me prove myself to you."

I flash back to the exact moment when this man stood between me and a madman with a gun and refused to budge. He risked his life for me. And he's *still here*, wanting more, wanting a life with me. I'm afraid to trust this, but I think he is the one.

My eyes tear up, and my throat is so tight all I can do is nod.

27

Jack

The next morning, we sleep in a bit, and then shower together before getting dressed and heading to Estes Park for brunch. I take her to the best little café I've ever been to for pancakes and coffee.

"Feel like going on a hike?" I ask her when we're just about done eating. "There's a lake not far from here. It's supposed to be nice. It gets good reviews." I show her the ratings on my phone screen.

She nods as she sips the last bit of her second cup of coffee. "Sure."

Lake Belleview is about as picturesque as lakes come. The water is crystal clear, and the undulating shoreline is punctuated by patches of sandy beaches, waving grasses, and shade trees. It looks like something you'd see on a postcard or a travel brochure. It's an easy three-mile hike around the perimeter, along a level, well-worn path.

The weather's mild, and it's a beautiful day. Fortunately, we seem to be the only ones on this path. The only other person here is a lone, middle-aged woman with dark, curly hair who's kayaking alone on the lake.

"We picked the right time," Ruth says, referring to the quiet.

I hold out my hand, and she takes it. We walk hand-in-hand for the entire three miles, neither one of us saying a word. We're just enjoying the scenery and each other's company.

When we reach the parking lot, Ruth steps up to me and kisses me. "Thank you for a perfect morning." She seems more relaxed than I've ever seen her.

I place my hands on her hips and pull her close. "My pleasure."

We're back in Bryce by two, in plenty of time to get

the tavern ready to open. I think back to what Ruth told me about her ex trying to pressure her into selling the bar, or at least letting someone else run it for her. If he didn't understand how important this place is to her—how integral it is to her sense of identity—he was a fool, and he got what he deserved. This place is more than just a business to her—it's her family legacy.

"Test me," I tell Ruth as we're standing at the bar. We just opened the doors, and customers are steadily filing in.

"How about... a fuzzy navel?" she suggests.

I roll my eyes at her. "Is that even a drink?"

"It is," she says. "Look it up."

I open Ruth's handmade, spiral-bound notebook and, sure enough, she has a recipe in here for a fuzzy navel. "That's just wrong," I say, but nevertheless, I collect the ingredients to make one.

It's not hard. Three ounces of Peach Schnapps, three ounces of fresh-squeezed orange juice, and ice. I mix the ingredients in a tumbler and pour into a glass.

"Don't forget the garnish," she says, pointing to a dish of fresh orange slices.

There seems to be an unusual number of young women lining up at the bar to place orders. Pretty soon, it's standing room only, as all the barstools are taken.

"What the hell's going on?" Tom asks as he takes in the surge of young women. "Is someone filming an episode of *The Bachelor?*"

I roll my eyes at Tom.

Ruth stands back, her arms crossed over her chest, and gives me an I-told-you-so look. "I said you could have your pick."

Shaking my head, I lean over and kiss her. "I already made my choice."

Around eight that night, Mike and Aleksa walk in through the rear entrance, surprising the hell out of me. They knew I was back in Bryce and planning to stay, but they never mentioned anything about coming out here again.

"Hey, guys!" I say when they walk up to the bar. I come around to greet them, giving them each a bear hug.

Ruth walks around the bar and hugs them as well. "It's good to see you guys again."

"What are you doing here?" I ask.

"We had to come see for ourselves," Mike says.

"See what?" I ask.

Mike gestures to me. "You, playing bartender."

"Hey, I'm pretty good at this. Try me."

Mike ponders a moment, then says, "How about a Blue Balls Shot. I'm *sure* you're familiar with that."

I ignore his comment about the color of my balls. "A what?"

"It's in the book," Ruth says, trying not to laugh.

It turns out that's an easy enough cocktail to make: coconut rum, Blue Curacao, Peach Schnapps, and sweet and sour. I mix one up and hand it to Mike. It's fluorescent blue.

"How about you?" I ask Aleksa.

Before he can even answer, a pretty blonde with curves that don't stop steps up to the bar and says, "I'll have a Pink Panty Dropper."

I check the book. Sure enough, it's in there—beer, vodka, tequila, and pink lemonade. I make a face as I mix the girl's drink. It sounds awful.

"So, how's he doing really?" Mike asks Ruth.

She's smiling as she watches me move on to the next customer's request. "Pretty well. As it turns out, he's more than just a pretty face."

Mike and Lexi end up getting a table, and before they know it, they've got a small group of girls hanging around them.

Ruth offers my friends dinner, on the house, and after

eating burgers and fries, they inform me they got a room at The Lone Wolf.

"So, you guys are planning to stay a while?" I ask.

"For a few days," Lexi says.

Mike knocks back the last of his beer. "Yeah, we're thinking about making a career change."

After we close up the bar that night, I walk Ruth to the back door. "Stay with me tonight?"

She nods. "I'd like that."

"Stay with me forever?"

She smiles. "I might be tempted."

Epilogue

Ruth
Three Months Later

I stand on the front porch of my cabin and watch Jack unload several cardboard boxes from the backseat of his Impala, along with his laptop bag and his oversized rucksack containing his small arsenal. He left most of the stuff he bought at the apartment for us to use there. But today, on one of our days off work, he's moving his personal items into my cabin.

Our cabin.

It's ours now, because Jack is moving in with me.

After having lived alone for so long, it's going to take

some time for me to get used to the idea.

"Are you sure you're ready for this?" Jack asks as he carries two boxes through the open door.

I follow him inside. "I'm sure."

And it's true. I *am* sure. I would never have agreed to let him move in if I wasn't. We've been pretty inseparable since Jack returned to Bryce. For the past few months, I've spent most of my nights with him in the apartment above the bar. It just made sense for him to move in here with me where we'd have more space and more privacy.

The more I know about this man, the deeper in love I fall. He seems to get me better than anyone ever has.

After setting the boxes down, he heads back outside to get the last of his stuff. He stops in front of me for a kiss. "How about I grill some steaks for dinner tonight? We could invite Micah to join us, if you want."

"That sounds like a great idea. Why don't you call him?" I love how Jack's been making a real effort to get to know my brother and spend time with him. They've developed a pretty easy friendship. He's gone up several times in Micah's helicopter, and Micah recently took Jack fishing up at Pine Lake on The Wilderness Lodge property.

Jack has integrated well into the community. He's

been on two more search and rescue missions with Hannah and Killian. Travis is giving him rock-climbing lessons, and he and Chris go to the shooting range together.

I never could have envisioned having someone in my life who got me, who didn't try to hem me in, or tell me what I should or shouldn't do. We fit together, like two puzzle pieces.

While Jack's finishing his unpacking—hanging his clothes in the closet in my bedroom—*our bedroom*—adding his man products to our bathroom, organizing his socks and underwear in the dresser drawers I cleared out for him, I go outside to the barn, grab my ax, and start chopping wood.

We're in winter now, and there's been snow on the ground for a couple of months. We're expecting a blizzard in a few days so I want to be sure I'm keeping up with the demand for firewood. We'll go through it about as fast as I can chop it.

I hear the snow crunching beneath his boots as Jack joins me. He's dressed in a brown suede winter coat, along with a knit hat and scarf, and a pair of winter work gloves. He watches me swing the ax for a few moments, then he picks up the logs scattered on the ground around me and carries them to the lean-to to begin stacking.

"Work up a good appetite," he says as I resume chopping. "I put some potatoes in the oven to go along with the steaks. We're having a meat and potatoes kind of evening. I invited Micah, by the way. He said yes."

The sun sets early this time of year. As darkness falls, I clean off my ax and store it in the barn. Then I go inside to help Jack with dinner.

While he's outside finishing off the steaks, I make a salad and put a loaf of bread in the oven.

I hear a knock on the door, and when I go to open it, Micah is standing there holding a six-pack of beer.

"Come on in," I say, stepping aside to let my brother in.

Micah stomps his boots on the welcome mat, knocking off chunks of snow. As he steps inside, he hands me the beer. "It's a housewarming present for Jack." He glances around. "Where is he?"

"Outside getting the steaks. Take your coat off and relax."

Micah hangs his winter parka on the coat rack and joins me in the kitchen. "So, how are you?" he asks, watching me intently.

"Fine." I stare back at him, starting to feel self-conscious. "Why do you ask?"

"Well, Jack's moving in. That's a big step for you. I just wondered if you were okay with it."

Smiling, I nod. "I am."

"So, do you anticipate wedding bells in your future?" he asks.

"Slow down, pal," I say with a chuckle. "He's just now moving in. One step at a time, okay?"

Jack walks in through the side door carrying a platter of perfectly seared steaks. When he spots my brother, he says, "Hey, Micah! Perfect timing. The steaks are ready. Have a seat."

While Jack sets the table, I pull the potatoes and the bread out of the oven.

"A toast," Micah says once we're all seated and eating. He lifts his bottle of beer. "To the two of you. I wish you the very best."

Jack taps his bottle to Micah's. "Thanks, man."

I catch Jack's eye, and he smiles at me. It's an intimate smile, reflecting all that we've shared and hinting at what the future will bring.

* * *

Later that night, as we're lying in bed, Jack and I make

love, taking our sweet time. He's a generous lover, so in tune with me and what I need. I turn the tables on him for a change, and with my hands and mouth, I make him squirm. When he finally surges into me, he's voracious.

Afterward, as we're cuddling, he turns to me and says, "Marry me, Ruth. Give me a chance to be the man I've always wanted to be—a man who deserves a woman like you. Deserves having a family with you. And if you'll give me that, I'll give you anything and everything you need."

Smiling, I brush his dark hair off his forehead. "That's a very pretty speech."

He grins. "I've been working on it a while now. How'd it sound?"

"Perfect."

"So, is that a yes?"

I raise my face to his and kiss him. "That's definitely a yes."

* * *

Thank you for reading *Dark and Dangerous*. I hope you enjoyed Ruth and Jack's story. Stay tuned for more books in the *McIntyre Search and Rescue* series.

* * *

If you'd like to receive free bonus content each month—exclusive for my newsletter subscribers—sign up for my newsletter on my website. You can also find links to my free short stories, information on upcoming releases, a reading order, and more.
www.aprilwilsonauthor.com

* * *

Here are links to my list of audiobooks:
www.aprilwilsonauthor.com/audiobooks

* * *

I interact daily with readers in my Facebook reader group (April Wilson Reader Group) where I post frequent updates and share teasers. Come join me!

Books by April Wilson

McIntyre Security Bodyguard Series:

Vulnerable

Fearless

Shane–a novella

Broken

Shattered

Imperfect

Ruined

Hostage

Redeemed

Marry Me–a novella

Snowbound–a novella

Regret

With This Ring–a novella

Collateral Damage

Special Delivery

Vanished

Baby Makes 3

McIntyre Security Bodyguard Series Box Sets:

Box Set 1

Box Set 2

Box Set 3

Box Set 4

McIntyre Security Protectors:
Finding Layla
Damaged Goods
Freeing Ruby

McIntyre Search and Rescue:
Search and Rescue
Lost and Found
Tattered and Torn
Dark and Dangerous

Tyler Jamison Novels:
Somebody to Love
Somebody to Hold
Somebody to Cherish

A British Billionaire Romance Series:
Charmed
Captivated

Miscellaneous Books:
Falling for His Bodyguard

* * *

Audiobooks by April Wilson

For links to my audiobooks, please visit my website:

www.aprilwilsonauthor.com/audiobooks

Printed in Great Britain
by Amazon